"Turn around and pretend you're walking,"

G.T. instructed her.

"Walking?"

"Yeah, I'll sneak up behind you and grab you, as if I were trying to mug you." Lordy, Lordy, just what he'd been trying to avoid these past few weeks.

"Oh, okay." Claire pivoted and used her hips to sashay away. "Like this?"

His eyes bugged out. No, not like that. Good grief, if she'd taken to walking like that, no wonder she expected to be dating soon. Any males in a ten-mile radius with better than twenty/two hundred vision would be following after her, panting and clutching at their chests. Forget the self-defense lessons. She needed to get a CPR certificate instead. G.T. thumped his own chest, trying to steady his heart's beat.

Dear Reader,

This month, Silhouette Romance presents an exciting new FABULOUS FATHER from Val Whisenand. Clay Ellis is *A Father Betrayed*—surprised to learn he has a child and has been deceived by the woman he'd always loved.

Long Lost Husband is a dramatic new romance from favorite author Joleen Daniels. Andrea Ballanger thought her ex-husband, Travis Hunter, had been killed in the line of duty. But then she learned Travis was very much alive....

Bachelor at the Wedding continues Sandra Steffen's heartwarming WEDDING WAGER series about three brothers who vow they'll never say "I do." This month, Kyle Harris loses the bet—and his heart—when he catches the wedding garter and falls for would-be bride Clarissa Cohagan.

Rounding out the month, you'll find love and laughter as a determined single mom tries to make herself over completely—much to the dismay of the man who loves her—in Terry Essig's *Hardheaded Woman*. In *The Baby Wish,* Myrna Mackenzie tells the touching story of a woman who longs to be a mother. Too bad her handsome boss has given up on family life—or so he thought.

And visit Sterling, Montana, for a delightful tale from Kara Larkin. There's a new doctor in town, and though he isn't planning on staying, pretty Deborah Pingree hopes he'll make some *Home Ties*.

Until next month, happy reading!

Anne Canadeo
Senior Editor
Silhouette Romance

Please address questions and book requests to:
Silhouette Reader Service
U.S.: 3010 Walden Ave., P.O. Box 1325, Buffalo, NY 14269
Canadian: P.O. Box 609, Fort Erie, Ont. L2A 5X3

HARDHEADED WOMAN

Terry Essig

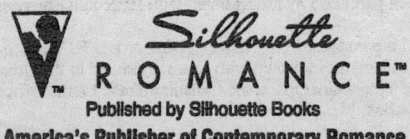

Published by Silhouette Books
America's Publisher of Contemporary Romance

If you purchased this book without a cover you should be aware that this book is stolen property. It was reported as "unsold and destroyed" to the publisher, and neither the author nor the publisher has received any payment for this "stripped book."

For my sister,
Mickey Parent Warnemeunde,
for all the Toaster and Maureen stories.

 SILHOUETTE BOOKS

ISBN 0-373-19044-1

HARDHEADED WOMAN

Copyright © 1994 by Terry Parent Essig

All rights reserved. Except for use in any review, the reproduction or utilization of this work in whole or in part in any form by any electronic, mechanical or other means, now known or hereafter invented, including xerography, photocopying and recording, or in any information storage or retrieval system, is forbidden without the written permission of the editorial office, Silhouette Books, 300 East 42nd Street, New York, NY 10017 U.S.A.

All characters in this book have no existence outside the imagination of the author and have no relation whatsoever to anyone bearing the same name or names. They are not even distantly inspired by any individual known or unknown to the author, and all incidents are pure invention.

This edition published by arrangement with Harlequin Enterprises B. V.

® and TM are trademarks of Harlequin Enterprises B. V., used under license. Trademarks indicated with ® are registered in the United States Patent and Trademark Office, the Canadian Trade Marks Office and in other countries.

Printed in U.S.A.

Books by Terry Essig

Silhouette Romance

House Calls #552
The Wedding March #662
Fearless Father #725
Housemates #1015
Hardheaded Woman #1044

Silhouette Special Edition

Father of the Brood #796

TERRY ESSIG

says that her writing is her escape valve from a life that leaves very little time for recreation or hobbies. With a husband and six young children, Terry works on her stories a little at a time, between seeing to her children's piano, sax and trombone lessons, their gymnastics, ice skating and swim team practices, and her own activities of leading a Brownie troop, participating in a car pool and attending organic chemistry classes. Her ideas, she says, come from her imagination and her life—neither one of which is lacking!

Chapter One

"So you want to tell me what the devil happened to your hair?"

Claire Martinson Greer defensively touched her short, cropped blond head. "You don't like it?" she asked her visitor.

"Well, if you were going for a change, you certainly succeeded," her ex-brother-in-law, G. T. Greer, allowed from where he lounged in a chair on the other side of Claire's small kitchen table.

Claire gave her head a small shake, then felt her hair. "I happen to like the way it falls right into place, no matter what you do. It's a very low-maintenance hairdo, which can be important to a mother of two young children."

"You never worried about low-maintenance hair before," G.T. reminded her. He dropped another chunk of warm home-baked muffin into his mouth and savored it. The woman made great muffins. No doubt about it. "And I don't buy it, anyway. You also changed the color. You can't tell me keeping it blond isn't going to require some effort. So come on, give. Who vandalized your head?"

Claire eyed him with disfavor. "Nobody vandalized my head. I tried dying it myself," she admitted with a sigh, "only it didn't quite work out. The hairdresser very graciously tried to fix it, but he said I'd fried the ends too badly and so he had to trim them for me."

"You lose, what, six, eight inches off the top of your head and call it a trim? And why blond? You had such nice brown hair."

Claire had it on her hairdresser's authority that her hair had been chestnut colored, not brown. But chestnut, she decided with a sniff, was probably not a tone a man was capable of defining. Only one type of *chest* anything was recognized by the male mind and *that* kind wasn't found on top of the head. Anyway, it no longer mattered. She was no longer a brunette of any sort, so she waved off his complaints with one hand. "Blondes have more fun. You're a man, you should know that."

Now that alarmed him. Claire had been more or less shell-shocked, he guessed would describe it, for the first twelve months after her divorce from his brother, Arnie. But lately she was showing some disturbing tendencies in the opposite direction. A delayed reaction, he supposed. Straightening up in his chair, he said, "Now, Claire, let's talk about this. You don't need to be dying your hair, or working out like a mad fiend with that step thing you bought, or torturing yourself in any way for that matter. You're just fine the way you are—were. Really nice, in fact."

Claire crinkled her nose while she tasted the word. "Nice? Did you say nice?" She shook her head. "I don't want to be *nice*. I want to be interesting—no, not interesting, *fascinating*. That's it. Fascinating. Alluring wouldn't be half-bad, either."

Lord save us all, thought G.T.

"In fact," Claire continued, "I'm thinking about going clothes shopping this weekend. I'm going to redo my wardrobe from head to toe, in reds and yellows."

G.T.'s brows rose as he thought of the change that would make from Claire's usual softly muted, understated clothing choices. "Why reds and yellows?" he asked. Admittedly he didn't know much about fashion, but he'd be surprised if Claire would look good in reds and yellows. Of course, a good, strong, brassy yellow would match her new hair. Was that good, fashionably speaking?

Claire defended her choice. "Red and yellow are bold," she told him. "And they're hot."

Bold and hot. Terrific. Sounded like the hooker he'd brought into the station for questioning last night. "I really think—"

"Did I tell you I'm thinking about applying to law school?"

G.T. blinked. A man could get dizzy just trying to keep up with the topic changes around here. "Law school?" he questioned carefully.

Claire leaned across her kitchen table and her animated hands went into overdrive. "Law has prestige. It's a highbrow, intellectual pursuit. Say you're a lawyer and immediately you're asked to serve on the local school board and to run for the village board of trustees. It's assumed that you're not only bright, but that you have something to offer—at least, that's what happened with Arnie. He served on so many committees, the kids practically needed an introduction when he actually stayed home for an evening."

"It's not a question of respect," her ex-brother-in-law, rather sourly informed her. "It's more like a question of money. They get asked to serve on every committee in sight in hopes they'll donate their legal expertise and save whatever group it is some *other* attorney's fees."

"That's another thing." Claire nodded brightly. "Lawyers actually make money worth discussing, unlike, say, elementary-school teachers if I chose to go back into education. Might as well pick something lucrative, don't you think?"

"Are you, by any chance, insinuating I made a bad career choice?" G.T. grunted as the sunlight beamed through the kitchen window and lit up the badge on the breast of his light blue uniform shirt.

"Could be," Claire answered seriously. "Cops certainly don't make much. But that's okay."

"Thanks. I'm glad my being broke meets with your approval."

"No, no. I just meant I'm not being pulled in that direction. I think I could be good at teaching, so it's too bad the pay is so terrible there, but I could never do police work. Some of the stuff you have to deal with on a day-to-day basis—I just don't see how you do it."

G.T. shrugged. "There are days when there's nothing like it on the face of the earth, and then there are other days when, well, all you can do is try not to take it too much to heart or you'd lose your mind. But take it from me. You'll never see me driving an expensive car. Not in this lifetime."

Claire rose from her seat and began clearing the table. "This will be good for me. Lawyers are aggressive, take-charge types. That's going to be the new me."

"Honey, I have to tell you, lawyers are not my favorite people in the whole world. At least, the ones I know seem to spend a great deal of time doing their best to undo every arrest I make, and besides, you haven't got an aggressive bone in your body," G.T. told her as he put his hand over the top of his coffee mug to protect it from her clearing. She immediately left it alone and he shook his head. Claire couldn't even take a cup away from an ex-relative who'd probably overstayed his welcome. Gelatin had more backbone than Claire. He couldn't imagine her in a courtroom, up against some slick legal eagle, brassy blond hair notwithstanding.

"I'll learn to be aggressive," she insisted, although it sounded as though she was trying to convince herself as well as G.T. "It's a dog-eat-dog world out there. Softness and mush just don't cut it. That part of my personality has to be excised, ruthlessly cut out. I've outgrown that naive, idealistic search for fulfillment and meaning in life. There is no meaning in life," she announced dramatically. "Life is a moldy bologna sandwich. Every day you take another bite. Then you know what happens?"

G.T. shook his head in morbid fascination.

Claire pointed her finger at him. "Then you die."

G.T. rolled his eyes to the ceiling and snorted.

"I'm serious," she insisted, which was exactly what he was afraid of.

"I no longer expect the Nobel prize when I solve world hunger. Now I just want a little respect. Arnie and your mother will be so impressed when I pull this off. He'll *have* to stop rolling his eyes every time I open my mouth when he's here visiting the kids."

"Arnie will never stop rolling his eyes, honey," G.T. informed her, hoping she'd missed his own ceiling search of a minute ago. "He was born rolling his eyes at the rest of us mere mortals. You'll never gain his respect because deciding you're a worthwhile person in your own right rather than just an appendage for him would mean admitting he'd made a mistake giving you up. And that ain't gonna happen. I lived with him a lot longer than you, and I know." Yes, sir. All his life he'd lived with him. G.T. had borne the brunt of Arnie's eye rolling for so many years he was amazed Arnie didn't have arthritis of the eye socket.

Claire looked at him thoughtfully, but her hesitation was brief. "No," she declared. "I have let the world act upon me long enough. I'm sick of being an act*ee*. Now it's time to be an act*or*. I can do this!" she announced resonantly to her audience of one.

G.T. covered his eyes with his hand for a brief moment of silent supplication. He didn't want her to see his eyes just then.

Claire went on. "I am going to knock the legal world dead, see if I don't."

"I think that's a crime," G.T. interjected mildly, but he doubted Claire heard him.

"I am an official smart person and I have the degrees and certificates to prove it. National Merit, Who's Who, Phi Beta Kappa. You name it and I earned it. I will whiz through this in record-breaking time. And when I'm done, I'll be invited into some prestigious law firm." Her eyes narrowed thoughtfully. "I'll have to find out which ones qualify around here." Then she shook her head and sent her brassy blond hair flying. "There's time for that, though. And when I'm there, I will have two, maybe three, assistants assigned just to me. And a secretary. I will be their mentor. They will look to me for their female role model. Together we will break through the glass ceiling. I can see it now." She paused in her task of putting away the muffins she'd just removed from the table.

G.T. could tell she was feeling guilty for being what she probably saw as inhospitable and he smiled when she guiltily offered, "Can I get you some more coffee? Another muffin?" Yes, that was his Claire.

"Let me finish this one first." G.T.'s crisp blue police uniform shirt rippled as he leaned forward to take a bite of the homemade apple muffin he'd snatched when she'd first removed the plate. "You're hopeless," he informed her as it practically melted in his mouth. Yeah, he could just see Claire smashing the glass ceiling. She'd probably bring a broom and dustpan for cleaning up the debris. "You know what I think? I think my big brother has a lot to answer for. The way he treated you while you were married is what's making you think there's something wrong with the way you are. There isn't. You were fine with brown hair. I liked it. And I like that pink thing you've got on, okay? I have difficulty seeing you in red." He sighed. "I can see it's not okay." Taking another bite to fortify himself, he reluctantly encouraged, "So tell me what you've got planned." Whatever it was, he already knew it was totally misguided. Fat lot Arnie cared about the havoc he'd wreaked around here. Obviously it was going to fall on G.T. to keep a close watch on Claire—just until she was back on an even keel, of course.

Although Claire was right about one thing. She was book smart. The classroom portion of learning the law would be a piece of cake for her. Heck, she'd had a college degree by the time she was twenty. Too bad it hadn't been in something a little more useful than Elizabethan literature.

Should have gone into something that would have forced her into contact with other people, he thought as he listened to the chair beneath him groan while he shifted positions. All that quiet reading stuff had only reinforced her basically introverted, shy personality. She'd probably been too inhibited to have an adolescence at the proper time, he decided. Now here she was, twenty-seven, and all hell was breaking loose. One of these days he was going to strangle Arnie for doing this to her. Then his eyes would really roll.

Maybe he could talk her into education. She'd been more on target there. She was good with kids. Schools were supposed to be nurturing environments, although the ones he'd attended had certainly missed the mark. Still, a twenty-seven-year-old adolescent rebel would probably survive better there than the legal arena. He just hoped she came out of this before she had her nose pierced or the rims of her ears decorated with studs. And while he thought he could handle the brassy blond hair color, if she progressed to green or purple streaks, he'd be forced to let her muddle through this rough patch on her own.

Darn it, why couldn't she have rebelled at sixteen like a normal person? Look at him. He'd shaved his high school's initials into his hair and painted half his face yellow and the other half black—the school colors—when the football team had made it to quarterfinals. And he'd only been fifteen! In terms of adolescence, he'd bloomed ahead of his time. Now that he thought about it, it had been freezing cold that night and he and his buddies had sat through the game shirtless. He bet Arnie had never done that!

Now if she'd only done something a little wild-haired like that at the proper time—heck, he'd have given her to seventeen, eighteen, even twenty, and called it close enough—she probably wouldn't have been so awestruck when his jerk of a brother had shown an interest in her, he reasoned. But, no. Arnold, his literally and figuratively fair-haired older brother had been able to feed his ego for quite some time on little else but the look of wonder in Claire's eyes every time she found him by her side.

"G.T.," Claire interrupted. "G.T., are you listening? I'm going to call Oakley University and start picking up some credits right away—this fall."

G.T. fiddled with his uniform cap while he debated how to proceed. How in the world had the woman reached the conclusion that metamorphosing herself into a hard-nosed egotistical slob like Arnie was either possible or admirable? He studied her face. No, she wasn't ready to hear anything he had to say. And for some reason best left unanalyzed, he truly didn't want her irritated with him.

He tried to be optimistic. Maybe she'd get suckered in by the female wrestling team and get this all out of her system in a couple of weeks' time. "If it's what you want, Claire, go for it," he found himself saying and prudently decided not to suggest wrestling as a way of meeting people on campus. A few extra college credits wouldn't kill her, he guessed. Wouldn't kill him, either, now that he thought about it. Hmm.

G.T. leaned back in his chair and stretched his long legs out in front of him. He watched as she leaned over the sink to see out the window. No doubt about it, Claire had the most magnificent line to her spine and neck—also her front—he'd ever seen. Far be it from him to put any ideas of modeling for the life-drawing class in her head as a way of picking up extra cash, although he'd bet she'd make one hell of a spectacular nude. He just hoped she didn't think of it herself.

"I was sixteen when I started college," she told him while she studied something outside he couldn't see.

He barely managed to prevent himself from throwing up his hands. See? It proved his point. She couldn't have had a proper adolescence. She'd already been out of high school at fifteen, for crying out loud. Criminal, that's what it was. And he couldn't help noticing some of her exuberance had faded.

"My parents took care of everything back then. Now I've thought this out as logically as I can and I'm sure this is the right path for me. This will sound stupid, but I don't know how to go about getting there from here. What do I do first?"

G.T. stood and juggled his cap. "I'd start with a phone call," he said.

"They'll laugh at me. Twenty-seven years old and clueless. It's embarrassing."

"They won't laugh," he assured her. "This is what people in an admissions office get paid for. They'll take one look at your transcript and trip all over their feet in delight at the prospect of adding you to their student body. Trust me." And if they didn't, he personally would point out their oversight. Or sign up for life drawing while mentioning what good money models made to Claire. Either or. Now where had *that* bit of perversion come from? He'd managed to shock himself—and him a policeman and therefore not easily shocked.

He palmed another muffin for the trip to the station—no reason to go by the doughnut place now—and deposited his mug in the sink. "Do it," he said. She was smart. She'd come to her senses on her own. He wouldn't have to say a thing. He'd just sort of stick close by for a while. No predatory male would take advantage of her while *he* was on duty. That's what ex-brother-in-law cops are for, he reminded himself virtuously. He plunked his uniform cap on his head.

"I don't know," she finally said. "The college I went to was so small, it got swallowed up by a nearby university. I may not even be able to get a transcript."

"Listen, ten seconds ago you were raring to go. Call." He grunted as he tugged the brim of his cap lower on his forehead and wondered where the brassy blonde had gone. All that was left of her fire now was the hair color itself. The swings of her personal pendulum were going to have him crazy in no time. "It's not a crime to ask. I'm a cop, I know these things." He stood and the kitchen immediately seemed smaller, such was his size. "I'm on duty at three. Do you need me to take a quick look at your checkbook before I take off?"

Quickly she shook her head in denial. "No. It's fine. I should have had Arnie show me how to balance it years ago. It's really not difficult at all, now that you've explained it all to me."

G.T. smiled gently. It was an odd expression on such a large man, she thought. Especially one sporting a gun, a club, handcuffs and a walkie-talkie. He'd always scared her a bit, but lately when he showed up at the door, she felt a bit of thrill work its way down her spine and that scared her even more. She was not interested in *any* man right now, let alone another Greer. She doubted if she would be ever again. Men were just too difficult to understand. Their minds worked along foreign neuron pathways, indecipherable to the average female. She'd thought this all through after her divorce, and if by some odd chance the unthinkable should happen—and she supposed that inexplicable male-female chemistry thing could strike twice—she would certainly fight it for all she was worth. Especially in the unlikely circumstances of it being a Greer brother. She'd *really* have to be stupid to do that.

She studied him consideringly. Oversized and intimidating, he was slightly smaller than his brother. G.T.'s features were marginally less regular than Arnie's, but unless you saw the siblings side by side, you'd never question G.T.'s good looks. In a way, his rugged features were far more appealing than Arnie's polished, plastic-looking image. If she hadn't learned her lesson about good-looking men, she certainly should have. As nearly as she could determine, G.T. was operating from the best of intentions, but she was absolutely going to learn to stand on her own two feet. That made it imperative to ease the man out of her life, not allow him to weave himself more intricately in. She sighed. In some ways, it really was too bad. Guess she'd have to learn to program the VCR by herself. And more than that, she actually enjoyed talking to him.

G.T. watched as Claire shied away the moment he stood. If it wouldn't give his mother a heart attack to disrupt the family harmony she cherished above all else, he'd beat his brother to a pulp, he thought rather grimly as he walked to the apartment's back kitchen door. He was careful not to crowd Claire as he made his way. The way he saw it, Arnie had crippled her by never making any attempt to teach her the everyday business of running a life. As far as G.T. was concerned, Arnie had known how protective Claire's parents had been. He'd known she'd been sent to small, private, all-girls schools all the way up to and through college.

That aura of protected innocence had been part of her appeal, he knew. Heck, he wasn't immune to it himself. But damn it, Arnie should have made some kind of effort to help her take charge of things. Now, somehow, it had fallen to him. He was tired of following along after Arnie and picking up his messes for him. Claire needed him, though, and he felt trapped in a web not of his own making. What was he? Some kind of expert on the female mind? Not. How the heck was he supposed to convince her to leave her hair alone and forget the red leather minis?

He reached for the doorknob without coming up with an answer and turned to Claire's sweetly upturned face. On some level Arnie had wanted to keep her dependent on him. Probably made him feel macho or something. But on another level he hadn't been able to handle the responsibility of such total dependency. He forced another smile. "Say hello to the two princesses for me when they wake up from their naps," he instructed her. "And call Oakley. Have them send out a course catalog." He stood there thoughtfully for a moment. "In fact, save it for me. I might want to take a look at it myself. Maybe it's time

I finished my own degree." Might as well accomplish something while he kept his eye on her. And it wasn't as if he hadn't been thinking about it, anyway.

Claire looked surprised. "You're twenty-eight years old, G.T. You've been happily at work for, what, seven or eight years? Why go back now?"

He fidgeted with the gun he wore at his waist, adjusting it a fraction of an inch. "There's very little upward mobility on a police force the size of Chicago's," he informed her. "Every time they give the sergeant's exam, I pass—along with several hundred of my closest buddies from the force. The list is always declared out-of-date long before my number comes up and the cycle starts over again. Maybe it's time to think about moving on." He leaned over and lightly kissed her forehead. Claire seemed too delicate for anything heavier. He couldn't imagine how she'd given birth—twice—let alone managed to get into a condition necessitating the birth process in the first place. She just seemed fragile, so delicate, to him.

He really was going to have to head off this shopping expedition. A vulnerable bombshell in bright red spandex to protect—just what he didn't need. He sighed. "I've got to go. I'll call you later in the week, see how things are going."

Claire watched as G.T. bounded down the three flights of stairs leading from the back of her apartment. Her fingertips touched the spot he'd kissed. Her forehead tingled there. She'd thought that part of her had died with her divorce. Darn it, it was *supposed* to have died with the divorce. And, by golly, it certainly seemed inappropriate for it to flare to life with her former brother-in-law, that was for sure. Not exactly immoral or anything, just somehow sort of improper.

One of those things you just knew the newspaper's columnist, Miss Etiquette, would heartily disapprove.

She craned her neck, but G.T. was gone from sight. Stepping back into the kitchen, she closed the door. There was no point in worrying about that spark of interest she felt. A man like G.T. would never be interested in her, anyway. She imagined the type of women he'd be attracted to—worldly, lean-and-mean types. Women police officers maybe, out in the world, fighting crime. Not a dumped, totally naive housewife, fighting grape-jelly stains in the laundry. She was fairly certain G.T. only came by because his mother was afraid of losing contact with her only grandchildren. Sending G.T. by a few times a week while only showing up herself Saturday mornings was, no doubt, Marilyn Greer's misguided notion of not appearing overwhelming.

Claire rinsed the coffee ring out of G.T.'s mug. Marilyn would lose interest as soon as Arnie remarried—his legal assistant seemed to be making progress in that direction—or G.T. took the plunge. It was odd, but the thought of G.T. doing something permanent hurt far more than Arnie's messing around on the job.

Her mind was certainly taking some odd turns lately. Claire shook her head to clear it and left the room to check on her two sleeping children. She'd just have to be careful. Make sure G.T. had no idea the effect those brotherly little pecks on the cheek and forehead had on her. Frankly, she doubted she could survive tangling with another Greer male. In point of fact, she had every intention of steering away from anything wearing pants—regardless of sex—for quite some time to come.

A soft smile lit up her whole face at the sight of her little girls laying curled on their sides, one cuddling a huge stuffed bear, the other a freckled fake-fur dalmatian puppy.

Claire's smile became a grin. Sound asleep and looking angelic, her children more than made up for everything she'd been through. There was the rare occasion when they were awake, however, she reminded herself as she eased the door shut again, when she had her doubts.

She cringed when the door clicked softly upon closing. Hard as it was to believe, there'd been five candles on Melissa's last birthday cake. Her naps were rapidly becoming unexpected treats to be treasured. Chrissie, on the other hand, had just turned three. She still slept so soundly each afternoon, Claire sometimes thought she'd be twenty-one before she gave up her nap. She listened outside the door a moment longer. Nothing. Good. She scurried back to the kitchen and pulled the phone book from a drawer. Maybe she could screw up enough courage to call the university before they woke up.

"The girls are going to grow up to be independent, capable, strong women," she told herself as she thumbed through the thin pages. "This is ridiculous to be in such a panic over every little thing. I never realized how everyone coddled me. The girls are going to know how to do things," she continued to mutter as she held her place in the phone book with one finger while punching numbers into the phone with its opposite. "I'll darn well see that they learn. Just as soon as I learn myself. So I screwed up my hair, big deal. A person has to take risks. No pain, no gain. Hello? Yes, I'd like to talk to somebody who can give me information on signing up for one of your classes, please. Yes. Thank you." See? She could do this. Piece of cake. So why was she suddenly sweating?

Chapter Two

"For crying out loud, Mom, it's midnight. What's going on? Somebody die?" G.T. sank tiredly down onto the edge of his bed and kicked off his shiny black shoes. He rolled his shoulders in a futile gesture to ease the ache there. One of his traffic stops had turned ugly. G.T. had collected a few new bruises before he'd been back in control. Traffic stops and domestic quarrels were the worst. You just never knew what you were getting into.

"I know what time it is, G.T. I also know you're not in bed. You couldn't have been home more than five or ten minutes, so stop acting like I've disturbed your beauty sleep."

"As usual, you're right, Mom. I did just get off duty. And I'm not in bed yet, but just as soon as I make a sandwich out of whatever I can find in my refrigerator that's not blue or fuzzy, I intend to crash. Now, keeping that in mind, what can I do for you?"

G.T. clamped the phone to his ear with a shoulder. That enabled him to listen while unbuttoning his shirt and stepping out of his pants.

His mother hesitated before responding. "Did something happen at work?" she finally asked.

"Just a drunk driver. Guy landed a couple before I got the cuffs on him."

"You're all right?"

"I'm tired of the jerks of the world using me for a punching bag, but other than that, yeah. I'm fine."

"Oh. Well, good. That's good that you're not hurt." Marilyn paused briefly before inquiring, "Uh, did you see the children? They haven't got the cold that's going around, do they?"

G.T. rolled his eyes before he could catch himself. Must be in the genes. And he should have known his being mauled by a belligerent drunk wouldn't overly concern his mother. It wasn't as if it had happened to Arnold, after all. "Yeah, I stopped by. And I don't know if they have colds, I didn't see them. They were both asleep. I'm sure Claire would have said something if they were sick, Mom. They were probably just worn out from running her ragged all morning."

"Claire looks exhausted? How will she watch the children if she gets sick?" His mother's voice squeaked in alarm.

G.T. tried not to groan as he pulled his shirt off. Damn, but his shoulder hurt. "Just kidding, Mom, just kidding. She looked fine." Other than her hair, that was. Deciding not to get into that, he sat on the bed once more and began stripping off his socks. "In fact, she was talking about going back to night school. Got her heart set on being a big-time lawyer."

He listened while his mother expressed concern over *that*. He found himself defending her choice and made a disgusted sound. "Get real, Mom. Of course I don't think the children will suffer if she leaves them two evenings a week. Perfect opportunity for them to spend quality time with their father," he put in a bit maliciously, knowing full well Arnie did his duty to his progeny every other weekend and kept busy with a cutie from his office in between. It probably irked him no end not to be able to simply stamp that wife-and-kids chapter of his life closed now that he'd declared it over.

He fumbled with his undershirt, pulling it over his head and losing the phone temporarily in the process. "What'd you say, Mom? You're going to have to speak up. I can't hear you." That would get her goat. Listening absently while his mother verbally worked her way through a long list of potential problems and their possible solutions, G.T. began sorting through the change he'd dropped on his dresser before he'd removed his pants. He'd found an Indian-head nickel only a month ago. Not very good condition, but, hey, it was something.

He started on the pennies. Might be something interesting there. Something mint condition would be nice. His fingers came to an abrupt halt as his mother's words registered. Interrupting hastily, he said, "No. Absolutely not. Ain't no way." He rolled his eyes as his mother continued, anyway. "Mother, I am not going to follow her out there every night in my squad and that's all there is to it."

Twenty-eight years old and his mother was still attempting to direct his life for him. Well, she could try. "Let's keep in mind I'm not the one who walked out on her, Mom. That was your other son. He's the one who should be feeling guilty, not me." He listened, but only momentarily. "My biorhythms are just fine, thank you. They do not need straightening out by switching to a day shift. I probably shouldn't tell you this, but even though my biorhythms are not messed I *am* switching to days. I'm going back to school, too." And he absolutely refused to admit Claire had anything to do with the decision.

While his mother orally digested *that,* G.T. attempted to put another wheel in motion. One that would alleviate a lot of potential problems he foresaw on the horizon. "Mom, you know that trip you've been thinking of taking to Hawaii? According to the papers, the airfare wars are really heating up right now and I bet Hawaii is beautiful in early September. Why don't you call your friend—you know, the one who's a travel agent? Hmm? No, no, of course I'm not trying to get rid of you. It was just a thought." And a damn good one at that. He'd have her gone within two weeks, count on it.

"Listen, I've got to go. I'm starved. Now if you promise to behave yourself, I'll try negotiating a deal with Claire where she leaves the girls with you the nights she goes to class." Until you hit the islands, that was. He hung up quickly and rambled out to his little kitchenette in his briefs to check out the refrigerator. As he attacked some leftover carryout chicken, he wondered what kind of mood Claire had been in tonight. Was her hair still brassy blond, or clown red at this point? Had she and the girls had meat loaf and mashed potatoes, or four-alarm chili with hot red peppers on the side? He'd have preferred either one to cold carryout chicken.

* * *

There was no time for second thoughts, Claire had discovered with her phone call. It was tough to fit in even first thoughts once the counselor she spoke to had informed her that registration for the fall semester was already going on. Classes, in fact, started up the third week of August. That had only given her two weeks to second-guess herself.

Those two weeks passed with distressing speed. G.T. came to dinner the night before classes were to start.

"You all ready for tomorrow night?" he asked as he stood by her side at the kitchen sink drying dishes.

No. She wasn't ready. But she was going, anyway. "I'm going tomorrow night even if it kills me," she told him. And that was a real possibility. The way her knees were shaking, she'd probably rattle some vital heart valve loose between now and then. Stupid thing would fall down her leg and bounce around inside her foot. The doctors would have a heck of a time retrieving it and getting it back in place. "I've been out of school seven years, G.T., and you know, I still wake up sometimes in the middle of the night covered with sweat."

"Yeah? Some kind of nightmare?"

"Term-paper nightmares. I dream I'm still in school and there's a paper due first thing in the morning that I'd forgotten about until just then."

G.T. put a stack of dried dinner plates up in the cabinet over Claire's head. "Yeah, majoring in English, you probably wrote a bunch of those."

"There was one semester where I wrote fifteen papers, most of them twenty pages long. But it's not always that. Sometimes I dream I've slept through a final after pulling an all-nighter studying for it."

"Yeah, I used to hate it when that happened."

"My heart will be pounding so hard, it takes a full five minutes to settle back down. I just wish the old memories could have faded a bit before I had to jump right back in."

He knew he should say something sympathetic, but all he could really think about was the flowery smell of hair and how much he'd have liked to be there when her heart was racing, maybe even contribute a bit to the problem, which was completely ridiculous. He needed to take a breather, he decided. Think about what was happening to him. "We're just about done here," he said. "If you don't mind, I'm going to go check on Chrissie. It's been a little while since we've seen her."

"You're right, it is a little too quiet around here. I'd appreciate your checking while I finish up. Missy, go pick out a story," she instructed her five-year-old daughter. "Maybe Uncle G.T. will read to you as soon as he checks on Chrissie."

"What book should I get, Mommy?"

Claire thought as she dunked a plastic tumbler into soapy water. "Hmm, we read *Mark's Trip to the Circus* last night. How about—" What was she doing? Probably the same thing her parents had done to her at this age. Wouldn't it be something if all her problems could be traced back to not being allowed to pick out good-night stories when she'd been five, and here she was doing it to her own child? *Mothers of the world, take note, lest generation after generation of milquetoasts and toastettes get their start at your nursery bookshelf.* Good grief, what a burden.

"You know what, sweetie?" she asked as she stacked the tumbler on the drain board and started fishing silverware out from the bottom of the sink full of water. "I think you're old enough to pick your own stories. In fact, I bet Chrissie can do it, too. You two surprise me, okay?"

Melissa's brow knit in concern. "Are you sure?" she asked. "What if I pick something you don't like?"

"Whatever you pick will be fine," she assured her.

"Well, do you feel like a store-bought book or one of the special ones you wrote for us?" Missy asked.

"My lips are sealed," Claire said with a smile. "I guess you'll just have to go see which one's calling your name." She managed to bite her tongue before she suggested the story she'd been thinking about earlier. But darn it, if Melissa couldn't even pick out a book now, what would she do when it came time to pick a career, a husband?

Missy wandered off, looking serious beneath the brown bangs she wore cropped at eyebrow length. Claire pulled the sink plug and shook suds off her hands before picking up her tea mug and sipping. If she finished it off before all the water escaped, she could wash it out and not have a single dirty dish in the sink.

She contemplated her predicament as she drank the tea. In the past two weeks, she'd accomplished a lot. The admissions counselor had informed her she could register by using a push-button phone and, by golly, she'd done it.

Civil procedure, criminal law and torts were all being offered evenings that semester, and Claire, exhausted by a process of trying to weigh the pros and cons of each class—she'd used a weighted point system that took as many variables as possible into consideration the way Arnie would have done—had finally given up and picked torts using, "Eenie meenie, mienie, moe." By hook or by crook, she'd worked her way through a series of recorded messages, used the asterisk and number-sign buttons for the first time in her life and it was done. She was registered for class. It had been a real pat-yourself-on-the-back kind of moment when she'd hung up. She'd taken care of photocopying her driver's license and sending that in as proof of residency, as well.

Right after that she'd gone to a bookstore and bought a book on family finance, using it to set up a budget for herself, and organized a file for receipts and bills. Now when G.T. stopped by as he was wont to do for no discernible reason, she made an effort to limit the time he spent with them to talk and horseplay with the girls. It would be all too easy to fall back into the trap of relying on a man, especially one like G.T. She was making progress, real progress, she decided.

But tomorrow night was the first class.

She couldn't go.

She had to go.

All right, all right. Think about this logically, she ordered herself. Go tomorrow night, and you're on your way. Besides, what's the worst that can happen? You might discover it's not for you, that you don't like it. Big deal.

Actually, that wasn't the worst. There was always the possibility of failure. Getting an F. It had been seven years since she'd last sat in a classroom, after all.

Maybe your brain has atrophied after five years of books with one-inch type. Maybe you'll ask stupid questions and everyone else will laugh.

"Claire," G.T. called, "you almost done in there? I've got a couple of good-looking women out here hot for some good-night stories."

"If you're willing to read to them, go ahead and start without me," she answered back. "I'll be there before you're done with the first book."

"Better hurry, Mommy," Chrissie advised in her high-pitched voice, "else Uncle G.T. might come and arrest you."

"Oooh, I'm really scared." Claire yelled so she could make her voice heard over the sound of the running water she was using to lazily swish soapsuds down the drain. She tried to inject a tremor or two into her voice to show her terror. "Now I'll really hurry," she assured them all.

Hurry out to G.T.? She could never explain to him about giving up before she'd even started. She'd have to go. *And you've always been good at book learning*, she reminded herself. It did little to bolster her spirits.

She didn't want G.T. to think less of her, either, and that made her mad. She shouldn't be thinking in those kinds of terms. Claire cleaned out her mug, then rinsed the rest of the suds down the drain. "There," she grumbled. "My sink is empty and tomorrow I'm going to Oakley and get started on a new, and this time *useful* career path."

Claire walked in the living room and flushed as she realized what G.T. was reading. It was one of the stories she'd written herself. Walking to the sofa, she squeezed herself in between G.T. and Melissa, intent on commandeering her manuscript. "Move over, you all." She gave G.T. an extra shove with her hip. "Especially you, Mr. Policeman. You're hogging all the space." Immediately she regretted her action as heat instantly spread through her body as it made contact with G.T. "Here, give me that. I'll finish reading it since you're in such a hurry."

But G.T. refused to relinquish it. "Nothing doing. This is good stuff. Missy says you wrote it just for them?"

"Not exactly," she muttered as she flushed. "I wrote it for a slightly larger audience than that."

"Yeah? Who?"

She reddened further. This was so stupid. "Try the children of the world. Unfortunately the publishers of the world weren't interested." And she must have been incredibly naive to think they would have been. Well, she'd learned her lesson. Now she was going for practical in her pursuits.

"Keep sending it out," G.T. advised. "It's really cute. Somebody'll buy it. It just takes a while to break into the market."

"More time than I've got in a single lifetime," Claire muttered under her breath as she switched places with Missy and pulled Chrissie onto her lap. G.T. finished the story and read two others before Claire declared the girls had to get to bed.

G.T. was waiting for her in the living room when she came back from tucking them in. "So. I guess torts starts tomorrow, huh?" he asked, thumbs hooked through the belt loops on his jeans.

"Tomorrow night, 6:00 p.m., room 262." She smiled a bit sickly.

"I've got tomorrow off. I'll come by. Take you out to Oakley earlier in the day for a dry run. We'll get you a parking sticker, see if the bookstore has a list of texts for the various classes, get the lay of the building. That kind of thing. Then you'll feel more at ease when you go for real tomorrow night."

It sounded wonderful. It would be marvelous to have him do that for her. "Don't worry about it, G.T. I'm all set."

He looked surprised. "You've got your sticker and your book?"

She crossed her fingers behind her back and nodded her head. "Yep."

"You got a campus map? You can find the classroom?"

"Sure I can." She'd take care of all that first thing in the morning. By herself.

"Oh. Well, then, I guess you don't need me for anything."

He sounded disappointed, which was silly, she told herself. "You know you're always welcome to come by and visit," she told him as she carefully led him to the door without touching him. "In fact, come for dinner on Wednesday. I'll tell you all about it."

Shortly after easing G.T. out the door, Claire rolled into her solitary bed and prayed for dawn, too keyed up to sleep. She just wanted tomorrow over with.

During Missy's morning kindergarten time, she took Chrissie out to Oakley with her.

"Come on, Chrissie. We'll go for a ride."

"Where we goin', Mommy?"

"To a school. A big school."

"Missy's?"

"No. A different school from Missy's. It's Mommy's new school."

Her three-year-old absorbed that while Claire buckled her into her car seat. "Mommy?"

"Yes, sweet cheeks?"

"I thought you knowed everything. What you going to school for?"

Claire stared at the child momentarily before answering, "No, lover bug, I don't know everything. I wish I did." In fact, she had her hands full at that very moment trying to figure out how in the world she was going to pick up her parking sticker. It seemed like one of those catch-22 situations to her. You had to park in order to go inside the building and get a parking sticker, but you needed a parking sticker in order to park. She'd probably get a ticket. Or worse, her car would be towed away and she'd spend the rest of the day trying to find it. It would have been nice to let G.T. take care of this for her. G.T. was, after all, a natural caretaker, and Claire, in some former life, had obviously doted on being taken care of—maybe she'd been a harem girl? Her eyes lit. That would mean she must have had a decent bust size back then. At any rate, that had been a past life and those tendencies of hers to cave in and let herself be taken care of would just have to stay back across time and in the harem.

Claire pulled her own shoulder harness across her chest and turned her key in the ignition. "Okay, snookers, here we go. We're off on another adventure as only Mom knows how to have them." Claire took a deep breath and backed cautiously out of her spot. All she had to do was get out to Oakley, find a place to leave the car where she wouldn't get a ticket while she went in to buy the parking sticker, get the textbook, find the classroom, avoid running into G.T. and get back in time for Melissa. No problem.

Grandma Marilyn showed up at five o'clock that afternoon. She was going to sit this week and next, then the fourteen-year-old next door would take over while Grandma went to Hawaii for a month. She came with her usual several bags of groceries, cellophane-wrapped sacks of treats peaking over the tops of every one of them. The girls loved it when Grandma showed up, and it wasn't one hundred percent due to the older woman's sparkling personality.

"How're my big girls?" she gushed as she came in with the first load. "I think you've grown just in the past few days."

Chrissie and Melissa beamed while they eyed the brown paper bags on the counter. Last time there'd been chips, animal crackers with pink icing, two kinds of candy—both with chocolate—and a plastic container with popcorn in Grandma's bags. "You're babysittin' us tonight, Grandma," they informed her.

"I know," she responded. "And we're going to have a lot of fun, too. I hope you two have a game all set up and ready to go. I'm in the mood to beat the pants off both of you."

"Aw, Grandma, you always say that. You always lose, anyway."

"This time it will be different," she assured them. "I can feel it in my bones."

"Yeah?" Missy inquired interestedly. "What do they feel like?"

"More importantly, you need to remember it's a school night for you, Miss Melissa," Claire warned as she took the textbook she'd purchased down from a high kitchen cabinet shelf. Crayon drawings and smudgy little fingerprints would not impress her classmates or professor, she was sure. "I want you in bed with lights out by eight-thirty. Do you both, I guess I should say all three of you, hear me?"

"Yes, Mommy," Missy responded.

"Okay," said Chrissie.

Marilyn agreed, too. "No problem."

The three of them looked at her with eyes far too innocent. She sighed, recognizing a lost proposition when she saw one. "I won't be back in time to kiss you good-night." She hoped. Surely Marilyn would have them asleep by ten-thirty. "So come get a hug now before I leave."

The girls responded enthusiastically and it was five more minutes before Claire made it out the door.

She concentrated on her driving, glad she'd built extra time into her schedule. Usually she was making dinner around now and the sheer volume of cars on the road at five-thirty caught her by surprise. But sooner than she wanted, the red pillar with Oakley scrawled up its side came into view and Claire turned left into the driveway it marked.

"This is actually a very pretty campus," she told herself as she wound her way through the heavily wooded front area. "Too bad I'm such a wreck I can't appreciate the scenery."

She was still talking to herself as she walked down yet another hall trying to find her classroom number. She'd run out of time that morning, but she'd naively assumed there'd be some sort of sequential order to the room numbers and it wouldn't be a problem. "How can 281 be next door to 257? I ask you now, how is this possible? What'd they do, hire some psycho to paint the numbers? Melissa could have done a better job. *Chrissie* could have done a better job. I don't think there even *is* a 262. And if there is and I don't find it in two seconds flat, I'm going home, anyway. This is ridiculous. I've never— Excuse me, would you happen to know where room 262 is?" Claire smiled winningly at a twelve-year-old girl masquerading as a college student. You knew you were getting old yourself when college kids looked like babies. When had it happened?

"This whole hall is odd numbers. Evens are over in that wing."

"Oh." See? Obviously only someone deeply disturbed could come up with this system. "Well, thank you very much." This was all G.T.'s fault. He should have talked her out of this. Next time she saw him, she'd wring his neck, provided she could get her hands around it.

"You're welcome, ma'am."

Ma'am. That little girl had called her ma'am. She was going home for sure. She didn't need this. People had managed to sue one another for years without her. They'd probably keep right on— There it was. Room 262. Oh, God, she'd found it.

She steeled herself and went in the open door. It was probably psychologically motivated, a subconscious unwillingness to totally commit to this class, she supposed, but she chose a seat at the end of a table halfway back in the room. It was the chair closest to the door.

Settling in, she glanced around. Maybe twelve to fifteen other students filled in spots at tables here and there. All of them looked younger, although two of them were professionally dressed and had obviously come in to class after a day on a job.

Claire checked her watch. It was six o'clock on the dot. *Okay, so let's get this show on the road.*

Chapter Three

The door opened and...G.T. slunk into the room, looking surly. He glanced around, then his eyes fell on her.

"G.T., what are you doing here?"

"You knew I was thinking of going back to school, finishing up my degree," he complained as he crossed his arms over his chest in a defensive posture. "You're the one who loaned me your course catalog."

"You're taking torts?"

"Of course not. This is a graduate-level class. Right now, I'm not thinking any further than a BA. Maybe in secondary education. I figure maybe I can use my police training to keep order in the classroom. Keep the troublemakers spread-eagled against the blackboard while I read grammar rules to them, if I have to." He shrugged. "Make a change from reading Miranda to criminals, I guess. At any rate, right now

I'm signed up for expository writing. It's a basic requirement for any kind of degree."

Claire thought about that. "Okay, so why are you here? It's six o'clock right now. You're going to be late. Can't you find your classroom?"

G.T. looked downright insulted at that. "Of course I can find my classroom. I'm a cop! I'm very good at following clues."

"Sorry."

"You should be," he growled.

"Well?" she prodded.

He looked decidedly uncomfortable. "Well, I just wanted to double-check on you first," he admitted reluctantly. "Make sure you got here okay and everything."

Claire thought of that harem girl she might have been in a former life and knew she'd have to work on being more assertive if she wasn't to be swallowed alive by the Greer family. "G.T., get out of here before I smack you one." There, how about that?

"Striking an officer of the law is a ticketable offense."

"G.T.—"

He held up his hands in a posture of capitulation. "All right, all right. I'm leaving." But he paused on his way back out the door. "Maybe our breaks will overlap. Come down to the cafeteria. If I'm there, I'll buy you a cup of coffee."

Her refusal stuck on the tip of her tongue. You know, big macho men couldn't admit to being nervous, of course, but it had been a lot longer since G.T. had seen the inside of a classroom than it had been for her. "Okay," she said before probing delicately, "everything all right?"

She all but recoiled when he burst out with a snarl. "No, nothing's all right. Does that make you feel better? I have no clue what I'm doing here. This plan stunk when you first planted the seed in my brain that afternoon in your kitchen and it's done nothing but ripen with time. And the really stupid part is that in order to put myself back at the scene of my worst nightmares, I've had to change duties and barter shifts like a crazy man. Look, I've got to go. I'll see you later. If we miss each other at break, wait for me here after class and I'll walk you to your car."

The door slammed behind him before she could tell him she'd be fine and not to bother.

Well! she thought as the professor finally showed up. Maybe she *ought* to let him walk her to her car. That way she could protect the rest of the student body from being mowed over. The man was in a snit and clearly not in any kind of mood to be messed with.

The words "Mr. Litcomb" were scrawled on the blackboard and the man began talking as he gave his papers one last shuffle. Claire took careful note of his office hours and his expectations for the class, her attention gradually engaged. Heck, it wasn't as though G.T. had insisted on driving her both ways. And the lot did appear a bit underlit. G.T. would probably have something to say about that. She smiled to herself.

"The word tort is a legal term referring to some kind of legal wrong for which you can expect to collect compensation for damages."

Hmm, was there anything on the books dealing with jerkiness? Could she sue Arnie for passing half-jerk genes down to her unsuspecting beautiful progeny?

Mr. Litcomb droned on for an hour and a half before he gave his papers one final shuffle and gave them a fifteen, he repeated, fifteen-minute break. Claire flexed her hand as she went in search of the cafeteria. She had severe writer's cramp.

G.T. was waiting by the food entrance. He sipped from one cup while holding another steaming paper cup in his other hand. Wordlessly, he offered it to her, then reached for the stack of books in her arms. "Come on, let's sit down. I really need this jolt of caffeine. I've been on the seven-to-three shift the past two days, but my body's still on last month's three to eleven schedule."

Claire refused to relinquish her book and notebook once she realized what G.T. intended. "Let go, G.T. I can carry them."

G.T. looked oddly hurt. "I know you're capable of carrying a book, Claire. I was merely trying to be polite—gentlemanly, you know? On the rare occasion, I do that."

Fine, make her feel petty. See if she cared. "Sorry, I just wanted to do things for myself."

He gave her a disgruntled look. "You sound like Chrissie."

"You mean like a three-year-old? Thanks a bunch." But darn it, she didn't want G.T. doing things for her. It would be too easy to allow him to dominate her the way his brother had. He was too large, too male, too attractive and too darned easy to give in to. Even now, he had her arm and was guiding her. They passed the food line and Claire stopped dead in her tracks. There, down by the end of the snaking line of students right next to the cashier was a small freezer case with several immediately recognizable and well-loved ice-cream bar labels advertised on the side. "Here, hold this," she said, holding out her coffee cup and books.

"Wait! Hold on, I don't have it yet." Desperately he tried to juggle what she'd thrust at him along with his own things. "What is with you?" he finally asked once he had a firm grip on everything in his arms. "One minute I'm not allowed to touch your precious notebooks and the next you're throwing them at me. Would you mind telling me what's going on?"

"I just realized I'm by myself," she explained.

"Oh, and what am I, the invisible man?"

She looked at him impatiently. "No, no, when a mother says that, she means there aren't any children around."

"Oh." He tried to sip his coffee and burned his tongue. He grimaced. "Good thing you explained that. I suppose it's something that at least you don't see me as a child. Maybe I could pay you to talk to my mother—think you could convince her I'm no longer a kid?"

But Claire was not interested in G.T.'s problems with his mother, not now. "Don't you see? Not only do I not have to set a good example—they'll never know I ate this ice-cream bar—but I can get away with only buying one, which is a whole lot cheaper than three of something expensive like this."

He straightened up at that. "Arnold is keeping up with his payments, isn't he?"

"The first of every month it's in my mailbox, along with the gas and electric bills. It's not that."

G.T. relaxed. He tried another cautious sip. He'd personally break a board over big brother's head if Arnie started missing payments. Arnie had gotten off on Claire's shy dependency—it was why he'd married her. It was hardly Claire's fault Arnie had changed his mind on what type of woman he found appealing. What he had to wonder was, had Arnie seen the new Claire? If he had, what did he think of his retiring violet's new flashiness? He'd better not be thinking of waltzing back into Claire's life and trying to pick up where he'd left off.

As far as G.T. was concerned, Arnie had had his chance and blown it. Claire deserved an opportunity to find happiness with somebody else, and G.T. considered it his civic responsibility to make sure Arnie or any other jerk, who couldn't see past a yellow spandex bodysuit and slim-fitting jeans to the real woman beneath, didn't rob her of that opportunity.

Then he thought about that and asked himself, why me? How did this get to be my job? He had no answer, so he glanced at his watch. "Go grab your ice cream. Then come tell me what bothers you about buying the three of you an occasional treat. But hurry, I've only got six minutes left."

Claire grinned, then sighed. One had to develop a sense of humor about life, or you'd darn well kill yourself. And it was funny, in an exasperating, unfunny sort of way. G.T. was just as protective of her as Arnie had initially been. She must still have a pigeon-with-a-clipped-wing look about her even with her new severely clipped hair and bolder clothing. Well, not for long. She'd set her plan in motion. The wounded little bird was about to become a glorious legal eagle. Female eagles were larger and fiercer than the males. They had a seven-foot wingspan, to boot. She knew; she'd looked it up. So take that, pigeons of the world!

She would metamorphose into an eagle if it killed her. But first, she had an illicit ice-cream bar to eat and explanations to make. She found G.T. at the table he'd chosen, sat down, unwrapped the ice-cream bar and took a bite. It was so cold it hurt her teeth. Mmm. "To get back to your question," she said as she savored the combination of vanilla and chocolate, "I believe Arnie should help support the kids, they're half his, after all."

"Damn right." He grunted as he finished his cup of coffee and started on the one he'd bought for her. Might as well; she obviously didn't appreciate it.

"But I don't feel comfortable wasting the money on expensive treats because they're mine, too. I should be contributing something, as well. And I will," she stated with more determination than she felt. "The girls and I won't be a millstone around the Greer neck forever, you'll see. A few years from now, I'll be ready to tell Arnie he can reduce his payments to just the child support and shove the alimony part."

G.T. sputtered into his coffee cup. Shy little mouse Claire was going to tell the big bad city lawyer to shove it? That would be a show worth buying a ticket to. "Uh, Claire, maybe we better talk—"

"Not now," Claire interrupted. She rose from her seat and gestured to the large clock she'd noticed hanging high on the cafeteria wall. "I have to get back."

G.T. glanced at his watch and jumped up. "Damn, I'm late." He quickly threaded his way through the congested table area, pushing Claire in front of him. He tossed his cup into the trash can guarding the exit, then caught up with her in the more open hallway.

"Claire, listen to me. You can't give up your money. You deserve it and—"

"Nobody deserves something for nothing. Arnie made a *mistake* thinking he could be happy with me, but he didn't commit a crime. At least, not one that's been covered so far this evening."

"Bull." The scars Arnie had left behind were nothing short of criminal, as far as G.T. was concerned. He was beginning to realize Claire might have extrapolated lessons never meant to be learned from her marriage to his big brother. In fact, he wondered if she wasn't thinking she was incapable of keeping any man content. "Now you listen to me. Arnie is a thirty-one-year-old immature jerk. He—"

Claire stopped dead in the hall. G.T. had to stop and turn back to her. The two girls behind them gave Claire a dirty look when they were forced to detour around them. G.T. outglowered them.

"What'd you stop for? You could have gotten hurt if those two had plowed into you," he lectured, loud enough for the girls to overhear.

"You ever ask yourself why you're so firmly on my side in all this?" she asked him, oblivious to the overweight duo's stares. "I mean, Arnie is your brother. You should be in his camp."

"Don't be ridiculous." G.T. snorted. "Arnie's a one-man army. He doesn't need me in his camp. The last thing he needs is defending or protecting."

"Don't you get it? In the normal course of events, you and your parents both should have me painted as the wicked witch of the west in this divorce. But instead, you all came down on poor Arnie like a ton of bricks. It was hardly *his* fault I couldn't make him happy."

G.T., who had just started walking again, stopped abruptly and stared at her. "That is without a doubt the single most asinine statement I have ever heard anyone make. And believe you me, after eight years of being a public servant, I have listened to my fair share of asinine remarks. Why, just this morning I ticketed a man whose excuse for speeding was that he was going to be late for his court appearance for his last ticket."

Claire, who'd been all set to be hurt by G.T. jumping all over her, giggled instead. "You're making that up. Nobody's that stupid."

"Oh, yeah? I pulled over a lady two days ago doing sixty in a forty. She told me she shouldn't get a ticket, that it wasn't her fault."

"And why was that?" Claire asked suspiciously.

G.T. shrugged. "She was only trying to get to a bathroom before she had an accident."

"No! She said that?"

He held up his right hand. "God's truth."

"Oh my gosh, how embarrassing for her."

G.T. took her arm and started her down the hall once more. "Embarrassing for her? What about me? I'm the one who had to stand there writing out the ticket, hoping she'd wait to explode until I was safely out of harm's way."

Primly, Claire entered the classroom. "You're being purposely disgusting," she said, but it was hard not to laugh.

G.T. was right behind her. "Oh, yeah? Well, you're the one hell bound and determined to spend the rest of your life wallowing in the mud with the cream of the local scuz. You will not believe some of the lowlifes you'll get to go to bat for if you become a public defender."

"Okay, so I won't be a public defender. Now, in case you didn't notice, you're late and you're in the wrong classroom. You better get a move on."

G.T. glanced at the watch on his wrist. "Damn. Well, they can just make do without me for a few more minutes. I'm not finished with you yet."

She rolled her eyes. "Listen, you can read me the riot act later. Mr. Litcomb's ready to start again. You may have written off your first night of class, but I'm not quite ready to give up so fast."

She settled into her seat and G.T. towered over her momentarily, looking frustrated. "Wait for me here when you're done," he finally growled. "You got that? Right here."

Claire waved her hand dismissively at him, and while his mouth worked silently for a brief time, no words escaped. She watched the classroom door close on him and released a breath she hadn't even been aware of holding. For her part, she had no intention of meekly waiting around after class like some speeder G.T. had pulled over and told to stay right there and wait for her ticket like a good little girl while he went and grabbed a second offender. Ridiculous. She focused her attention on the professor.

An hour later, she stretched and gratefully closed her notebook. At the rate this guy was going, she'd have to go out and buy a gross of the things. The man knew how to talk. Actually, he'd reminded her a bit of Arnie—full of obscure, long words and hot air. Slinging the strap of her purse across her shoulder, she left the classroom feeling a bit unsettled.

G.T. caught up with her halfway down the corridor. "Claire, wait!"

She glanced back over her shoulder. "Oh, hi."

He gave her a curious look. "'Oh, hi?' I thought you were going to wait for me back there." He gestured down the hall.

She began walking again as soon as he'd caught up. "No, I was directed to wait, but I never actually agreed to do so. There is a difference. I'm capable of finding my car all by myself."

G.T. sighed. It was hard to protect a woman bound and determined on a course of independence she really wasn't quite ready for. Especially one as prickly as Claire. So maybe he hadn't been as tactful as possible. He'd been thinking of her, hadn't he? Obviously that didn't count for much. "Okay," he began, "is it all right for me to ask where you parked your car? Maybe they're close to each other. Then it would be all right to walk together, wouldn't it?"

She thought about that. "I guess so. I'm in the lot off of Central Street."

G.T. hid a grimace. He was in the one on the opposite side of the campus off of Golf Road.

"Where are you?"

He responded quickly. "Oh, same as you. Did you get here early enough to get a spot close up?" He hoped, he hoped.

"Not really. But there are plenty of other cars around me and I did park under one of the overhead lights."

He bit back a sigh. He'd chased some punk close to a mile early that afternoon. Lost him when he'd gone over a fence. Without knowing what was waiting on the opposite side, G.T. had been forced to let him go, but his feet weren't being nearly as philosophical. They hurt. Why didn't they let cops wear sport shoes? "I had to park towards the back myself" was all he said.

"Good thing I parked under a light, huh?" Claire asked when they reached her car. "I can't believe how dark it is out here. And look how the lot has cleared out, too."

He'd rather not be reminded of how vulnerable Claire would be out here if there ever came a night he couldn't make it.

Claire glanced around as she unlocked her door. "Where's your car, G.T.? I don't see it."

He gestured vaguely. "It's around. Not too far."

"I don't see it," she repeated. "Want me to give you a lift to it?"

"Uh, no. Thanks, though." She'd only be royally ticked if she discovered it was at least a half a mile away. "I can use the exercise. Keep your doors locked and your windows up on the way home, all right? And say hello for me to those two monkeys you're raising when you see them in the morning."

"I'm not raising monkeys," she protested automatically.

He snorted. "Yeah, right. That's why I have footprints up my chest, over the top of my head and down my back." He closed her door for her.

Claire rolled down the window. "G.T.?"

He leaned down. "Yeah?"

"I—are you sure you don't want a ride to your car?"

He stood back up and stretched. "No, you just get going so Mom doesn't have time to totally corrupt the two monsters."

Claire looked up at him. "Yes, I guess I'd better at that." She hesitated, though. "I know this wouldn't be terribly macho to admit—Arnie would certainly never own up to being lost—but, G.T., you didn't forget where you parked your car, did you? Honestly, I wouldn't mind driving you around to look for it."

"I promise I can find it." G.T. brought two fingers to his lips, then touched them to hers. "Go on. Go."

Claire watched him a moment longer, then put the car in gear. "Right. See you Thursday night."

"Right. Thursday night." He stepped back from the car and gestured for her to leave. "Roll up your window," he yelled after her departing car. "Put on your air conditioning if you're hot. And lock your door!"

He began the long trek to the other side of the campus.

Chapter Four

"Did you have fun with Grandma?" Claire asked her two daughters over their bowls of oatmeal the next morning.

"Yeah, it was great," Melissa confirmed.

"Grandma taked her teeth out for us," Chrissie told her mother with relish. Clearly that event marked the high water of Grandma's visit.

Claire cringed and decided to ignore the comment. "I just hope you two were good for her."

"Oh, we were," Melissa affirmed. "Good as gold. Grandma even said."

"Yes, and she gived us golden money, we was so good," Chrissie remembered, her tone awed.

"Chocolate," Melissa added importantly. "Chocolate money all wrapped up in gold foil. Lots of it in a really neato little bag made of gold net, Grandma said. I saved mine for show-and-tell."

Well, at least they hadn't eaten everything in the three bags of junk food Grandma had shown up with last night. She supposed she ought to be grateful for that. "Sounds like your friends at school will all be impressed," she told Melissa while she idly stirred her cereal. "Where'd you put it for safekeeping? You didn't leave it in your pants pocket when you put your clothes in the laundry hamper, did you?"

"Oh, no. I don't put anything in my pocket since you got mad about the crayon melting in the dryer."

"Good. Where is it?"

"On the refrigerator next to the jelly. Grandma put it there."

"Very good," Claire said. She'd have to remember to thank Marilyn for that bit of wisdom. In fact, she wouldn't even mention the false teeth trick.

The dishes done, she and Chrissie walked Melissa the two blocks to her school and waved back as the child paused at the main entrance to vigorously pump her hand up and down in their direction.

Then she came back and sat at the kitchen table with a freshly brewed cup of tea and her law book while Chrissie watched a children's program on TV. Claire thought about G.T. rather than the torts text in front of her.

He puzzled her. In some respects, he was the antithesis of his brother. Arnold Greer had probably been born knowing what he wanted from life. By the time he was a couple of weeks old, he'd probably formulated his plan for achieving his life's goals and had been busily following that blueprint for the past thirty-one years. Claire suspected she'd been written off as nothing but a brief aberration on Arnie's path to success. One he'd quickly corrected for and gone on.

G.T., on the other hand, didn't seem to have any great aspirations. "I wonder," she asked herself as she tapped a pencil reflexively against her text, "if he always wanted to be a policeman, or if he just sort of fell into it when he decided not to finish college right away?"

She glanced down to the book's minute black type, then back up. She spoke to the overhead light bulb. "And I wonder why he's suddenly decided to do something different."

"Mom?"

"Hmm?"

"My show's doned."

"Okay, sugar pie. I have some studying to do, so I can't read to you right this minute. How about if I get out your watercolor paints? You haven't done that for a while."

Chrissie climbed up into the chair next to Claire's. "Let's bake cookies without Missy."

"That wouldn't be very nice. Maybe we'll do it after we pick her up later on."

Leaning over to study the open text, Chrissie declared, "Missy's a piglet. She don't share. I never get a turn to stir when she's here." Her face now in the book, Chrissie pointed with a pudgy little finger. "Who's those guys, Mom?"

"A bunch of old men arguing a point of law."

"Oh. They look mad."

"They do, don't they?"

"They better be careful. Uncle G.T. might under arrest them and put them in their rooms for a 'time out.'"

"It's an interesting thought, doll face."

"Grandma says Uncle G.T. went to your school last night, too."

"Yep, he sure did."

"Is he gonna learn to argue the...argue the...what you're learnin', too?"

Claire thought about that and again wondered exactly what G.T. had had in mind when he'd registered to go back to school. Did he have a goal in mind? She assumed he'd been kidding about using his police training to teach high school. You know, somebody ought to make sure this didn't turn into a wasted effort. Maybe she'd just elect herself to a committee of one and oversee the task. After all, he'd certainly gone out of his way to help her after the divorce. Still was, in fact. "You know what? I'm not sure what Uncle G.T.'s got on his mind. Maybe I'll try to talk to him tonight and find out," she told her tot.

"Grandma said he was taking a writing class, but that would be silly. He already knows how to write. I've seed him do it lots of times."

"Not that kind of writing, sweetness."

"What kind, then?" Chrissie demanded.

"Uh, a different kind." Claire shut her book. "Listen, kiddo. Tell you what. I guess I can do this later. Last night I thought up a new adventure for Toaster Beady and Maureen Schneider on my way home from class. Let's go sit on the sofa and I'll tell you all about it. Then, if you like it, we'll write it down like the others."

Chrissie loved Toaster and Maureen's rather adversarial trip to the dentist. She spent the remainder of the morning happily drawing crayon pictures to illustrate the text Claire entered into the computer and carefully printed out in large-size type.

After picking up Melissa from school and gobbling down leftover spaghetti for lunch, the three of them baked peanut-butter cookies. Chrissie had wanted chocolate chip, but Claire figured peanut-butter cookies at least had an excuse for being, however flimsy, and she tried to compensate by making sure Chrissie got a chance to stir.

Then it was the girls' quiet time. Claire went back to her text at the kitchen table while they rested, but she couldn't concentrate. "What is wrong with me?" she moaned as she found herself jumping out of her chair for the third time. "The girls will be up before you know it. I've got class again tomorrow night and I haven't gotten a stinking thing done. This is ridiculous," she muttered as she paced through the apartment's small living room, aimlessly picking up game pieces, hair bows and puzzle parts.

The lace curtains hanging in the living room windows flapped lightly in a sultry late-summer breeze. Claire leaned forward over the sofa to adjust them just as a familiar maroon car pulled into the curb on the street down below. Suddenly she knew why she'd been feeling edgy. G.T.'s shift had ended half an hour ago. On some level, she'd been waiting to see if he'd show up.

She pushed the window farther up and stuck her head out. "Hey," she called down, "that's not a legal spot. Wouldn't it be embarrassing for a policeman to get a parking ticket?"

G.T. flashed a smile that made her blink, and that from three stories up. "Watch this," he advised, and Claire was spellbound to do so.

G.T. didn't walk—Claire wasn't sure he was capable of a mere walk. He sauntered across the street to another illegally parked vehicle and pulled the ticket out from under the windshield wiper. Returning to his own car, he tucked it under his own blade, stepped back to inspect it, then readjusted the angle of the ticket to suit himself. Then he headed for the sidewalk in front of Claire's building. "There," he called up. "When the guy comes back down this block, he'll think he's already ticketed me. Happy? Now buzz me in."

Happy? Of course she wasn't happy. She was sure what he'd done had to be illegal. Fraud or something. How could he have—

"Hi," G.T. said as he finished bounding up the stairs with far too much energy for a man who'd just worked a full shift. "Where are the rest of my women?"

Then he kissed her. It was as always before, a buss on the cheek, but it unnerved her this time. It *tingled* when he did that now. She was pretty sure she didn't care for the sensation, pretty sure she didn't want to be referred to as "one of his women." She'd have to make sure to remember the lessons she'd learned from Arnie. One of them being to set her goals, then single-mindedly pursue them. Any involvement with G.T., however superficial, would only cloud the light she was determined to follow. She was going to be a hot-shot lawyer. The lady in yellow who single-handedly smashed the glass ceiling.

Forcing herself to breathe regularly, she stepped backward, increasing the distance between them. "You know the girls take a nap in the afternoon."

"Oh, yeah, I forgot."

"Well, they're asleep."

They stood in the narrow confines of the apartment's small front hall and looked at each other.

"So. How long have they been asleep?"

Claire glanced at her wrist. "About an hour, I guess."

"Oh, well, then, we better wake them up, huh? Otherwise they'll be up all night." He looked at her expectantly. "I want to go do something."

The man fairly vibrated with energy. It was disgusting. Who needed this? Just *thinking* about him had prevented her from getting any studying done all morning and afternoon and now he was in the flesh, ready to ruin her evening, as well. "G.T., why are you here?" she finally asked.

That seemed to stump him. "Do I have to have a reason?" he asked.

She slitted her eyes while she thought. "Yes," she decided.

"Well, I don't. It was sort of a spur-of-the-moment kind of thing. I thought if you weren't doing anything we could take the girls to the park or something."

She eyed him suspiciously. "You were so hot to go to the park with a three- and five-year-old you couldn't even take the time to go home and change out of your cop uniform? You're wearing a gun and handcuffs, for crying out loud."

"Well, I—"

"You're checking up on me, aren't you, G.T.?"

"Don't be silly. I told you—"

"Mommy, who're you talking to?"

"Uncle G.T.'s here, Missy, isn't that nice? He wants to play at the park. Is Chrissie awake, too?"

Melissa came through the living room, her stuffed-dalmatian sleeping companion under one arm, and met them in the front hall. "Yeah, she's awake. She snitched some cookies and took them into bed with her so she wouldn't be bored during nap time, only then she fell asleep on top of some she didn't have time to eat before she got tired, so she's trying to scrape all the crumbs out of her bed before you see them," the five-year-old reported matter-of-factly and without taking a breath.

"Terrific," Claire muttered. "I guess I better get in there before she grinds the crumbs into the carpet."

G.T. breathed a silent prayer of thanksgiving when she left the room. Damn it, he *hadn't* come to check up on her—he didn't think. Of course, that left coming just to see her as the reason he'd stopped, which couldn't be right, either. No, he was sure he'd come to take the three of them to the park. It was a beautiful afternoon, even if it was rather late in the day at this point. The girls should get some sunshine. Yes. September first came in just two more days. That made it practically fall, which came right before winter. The little ones should be thinking in terms of storing vitamin D for the shorter daylight hours that were obviously just around the corner, that was it.

"You really want to play at the park, Uncle G.T.?" Melissa asked.

He scooped her up into his arms. "You betcha. I had trouble concentrating on catching the bad guys today 'cause I kept thinking about how much I wanted to go swing instead."

Missy giggled in delight. "That's silly. You're too big to swing. Grown-ups don't really play at the park.

They just sit around on the benches and watch the kids have fun."

G.T. scowled at that. He'd spent most of his life watching—usually Arnie excelling at whatever he was doing while his parents oohed and aahed, and then almost but never quite duplicating the feat when his turn came three years later and he reached a similar age. "I was going to use you two girls as my cover. Pretend like I was taking you guys to the park, when really you were taking me. What do you think?"

Melissa appeared doubtful. "I won't have to push you on the swing, will I?"

"I can pump all by myself," G.T. informed her proudly. "All you'll have to do is stand back and applaud."

Melissa's eyes narrowed suspiciously. "Are you gonna hog the swings the whole time?"

"Is she your daughter, or what?" G.T. asked in aside to Claire who grinned ruefully in return.

"I'm not as bad as all that," Claire returned as she retrieved the girls' sneakers from the top of the television and moved to help them put the shoes on. "And a woman needs to be cautious in this day and age or she can get herself into all kinds of trouble."

"Why don't we just send her to law school now and save time? She's going to have me signing some kind of legal contract for what is and isn't acceptable on the playground in a few seconds." He lowered Melissa into a chair so her mother could wrestle her shoes on. "Tell you what. My wristwatch has a stopwatch built into it. We'll time our turns. How's that?"

"Well—okay."

"Thank God." G.T. wiped his brow in mock relief. "I gotta tell you, kiddo, you are one tough negotiator."

"What's a ne-ne—"

"Somebody who makes sure things are fair and square."

Melissa preened at that. "Oh, well, that's good, then."

"Sure it is," G.T. agreed. He glanced around the room. "Now do we need anything else for our trip to the park or are we all set?"

"It would be good if we bringed some juice boxes and cookies, case we getted hungry," Chrissie suggested as she played with her mother's fingers.

"Honey bunch, we're not going that far," Claire objected. "And the bees are out in full force this time of year. They'll be all over us."

"Uncle G.T. will come and arrest them. Please?" Chrissie pleaded.

"Yeah, Claire, no sweat. I'll protect you. I'll handcuff the little beggars and haul them off to the clink if they so much as put a toe across the park boundary."

Melissa laughed. "Bees don't got toes, Uncle G.T."

"Yeah," Chrissie chimed in, "and your handcuffs would be much too big for a bee. They're *little.*"

G.T. pretended to think about that. "Hmm, you might be right, but don't worry. I'll think of something. I'd never let anything happen to my three best women."

And Claire believed him. Oh, not that they were his three best women, but that he would always do his best to protect them, for as long as he thought they needed it. He was a natural born caretaker who would someday want a wife and children of his own. She had to be careful not to mistake his natural protectiveness for anything more meaningful—which was just fine, of course, since she was absolutely not interested in anything deeper. "Well, all right. Missy, run get the backpack. We've still got some peanut-butter cookies left and I think there are just enough juice boxes left to go around." Apple juice, as she recalled. That was a big bee drawer. It ought to be interesting watching G.T. duel with a swarm of those.

Of course, she conceded as she loaded up the backpack a few minutes later, G.T. in full uniform was a rather awesome sight. She could just catch sight of him from here. All she knew for sure was that G.T. had one impressive pair of shoulders, muscular arms, slim hips and terrifically long legs. There was every possibility the bees *would* take one look at him, turn tail and run for the nearest hive. God knew she felt like doing just that.

Unfortunately that wasn't a real option here, so instead of running for cover, she picked up the backpack and marched herself out to the living room. "All right. I'm all set to go. I can't think of anything else we might need, so let's blow this joint." She dropped her door key into her jeans' pocket and pulled open the front door.

"Uncle G.T., will you teach me how to pump?"

"Sure, pumpkin."

"Mom, let's bring the new storybook with us. You know. The one you and me writed this morning."

"What new storybook?" G.T. inquired interestedly.

"Mommy writed a great new story 'bout Toaster and Maureen, and I drawed the pictures," Chrissie informed G.T. proudly. "It's really good—all about their 'ventures at the dentist."

"Is that right?"

"Yeah, the bestest part is when the cavity inside Toaster's tooth is arguing with the dentist 'bout whether he has to get out of there or not."

"Who wins?" G.T. asked.

Claire was starting to feel flustered. It was just a silly story, like dozens of others she'd written. "Never mind who wins," she told G.T. a little more severely than was warranted. "We need to leave. It's going to be pitch-dark by the time we get to the park at the rate we're going."

"But I want to bring the story," Chrissie insisted.

"Why, sweetheart?" her mother asked, feeling a bit exasperated. "There're so many things to play on at the park, we don't need a book. We can read it when we get back."

"No." And it was a very emphatic negative, too. "I want to give it to the mailman, like we did last time."

"Why do you want to give your Mom's story to the mailman?" G.T. asked, slightly bewildered.

"So he can take it to New York."

"New York?"

Melissa explained. "We always give the mailman Mom's stories to take to New York. But the story people there are very mean and send them back. But Chrissie's right. I bet they'd like *this* one. I bet they'd turn *this* one into a real book with a cover and everything. One we could go to the store to see."

"Oh, well, if that's the case, Claire, you'd better go get it."

"G.T., this is silly," Claire objected. "I could probably put one of the girls through college with what I've paid out on postage to New York—and all to no avail, I might add. Why waste any more money on something that's just not going to happen?"

"My, my, what negative thinking."

"Please, Mommy?"

G.T. continued sanctimoniously, "Why, even now these two young children might be absorbing this quitter's philosophy into their subconscious psyches where it will take root and grow silently for years to come. Then suddenly, out of the blue, it will pop out on them, causing them to give up halfway through something really important—like their SATs or something—all because you refused to mail this one manuscript when they were young."

Claire socked him in the arm, hard.

"Ow! Now they'll grow up to be husband beaters."

"You're not my husband." She glared at him. "All right, all right. I'll get the stupid thing."

"It's not stupid, Mommy. Those are my bestest drawings ever."

Claire thought about sending some sophisticated New York editor a manuscript covered with childish crayonings and shuddered inside herself. Her options were limited. She could either crush her daughter's feelings or blow whatever slim chance of a sale she might have. She opted to blow the sale. "Chrissie, all I can say is, if they don't make a book out of this just for your pictures alone, they have holes in their little pointed heads."

"They must have holes in their heads," G.T. inserted smoothly. "After all, they haven't bought any of your mother's books, have they?"

"No."

"That proves it, then. Obviously their brains have all leaked out. That it?" He nodded at the small sheaf of papers Claire had picked up from the end table next to the living room sofa.

"Yes, such as it is."

G.T. ushered them all out the door. "Now, now, none of that. I read an article in the dentist's waiting room once by a lady who swears she wins contests and lotteries by positive thinking. She imagines herself the winner, sees herself soaking up the rays on Waikiki and *baboom*, next thing she knows, the phone's ringing."

Claire nodded her head sagely. "And the very next day she's packing her bikinis for a week in the sun."

He beamed at her. "Exactly. Although, truth be told, judging by the picture accompanying the article, I can only hope she went for a one-piece job with a loose top and one of those little skirt things rather than a bikini, but you've got the idea." He held the apartment building's front door open for the three of them and followed them out into the late-afternoon sunshine. "Now, the thing to do here is for the four of us to march on down to the post office and send this thing off with lots of good vibes."

"You're crazy." Claire blinked against the bright sun, but what a great afternoon. She could almost believe good things were going to come her way.

G.T. put a companionable arm around her shoulder while he expounded on his dentist waiting-room theory. "This time when you fork over the postage, we're all going to imagine that manuscript winging it's way to New York on a 747, or whatever plane's top of the line now."

"We're going to pay to send it by air?"

"Absolutely. Once in New York, we will picture it landing on some very receptive editor's desk."

Claire thought of the crayon drawings. "Yeah, right."

But G.T. was on a roll. "Then we will see ourselves going into a bookstore—I know, the one in the mall, where we will find an entire stack of them in the section for new releases."

Claire smiled wistfully. "Sounds good to me."

It sounded good to her kids, as well. "Let's do it, Mommy," Melissa entreated, excitement shimmering off her in waves.

Chrissie danced around their feet. "Will it have a cover and everything, Uncle G.T.?"

"You betcha, kiddo. A cover with a big picture of Toaster and Maureen."

"Oh, Mom, come on. This will be the best ever."

She knew she ought to caution them, not allow G.T. to set them up for disappointment like this, but their enthusiasm was contagious. She found herself agreeing. "I guess it won't hurt to give the literary world one last chance at publishing greatness."

"There you go." G.T. smiled approvingly.

She happened to have a form letter in her computer that she used for all her submissions. She just typed in the date and the name and address of the publisher and printed it. The manuscript was ready to go.

They found the post office right where it had always been—at the end of the block halfway between the apartment building and the park. Claire bought a padded envelope and wouldn't let the clerk meter it. She bought stamps featuring a heart and the word "love" instead. "Subliminal suggestion," she informed G.T. as she licked them and stuck them on the brown manila. "They will see these love stamps and their subconscious minds will know they are to love the manuscript that came with them."

"Good thinking," G.T. said approvingly. "I like your style."

She doubted the editor would. He never had before, but she didn't say that. The letdown would come soon enough. She handed the envelope back to the postman.

"Wait," G.T. said, and everyone in the place turned around to see why the policeman sounded so urgent.

Probably thought he'd just caught her in some kind of clever sting operation, Claire thought in disgust and asked, "What's the matter now?"

"Did you picture the 747?"

"G.T.—"

"Put your fingers here." He grabbed her hand and placed it on the envelope. "Yes, slightly left of center. That's the heart of the manuscript. Come on, kids. Everybody put your hand on top of your mother's, close your eyes and wish the book good journey and good luck."

Claire shook her head in mock despair at his silliness, but she did as she was told. The clerk took the padded envelope from the girls, touched its center with two fingertips before winking at the two little ones, then tossed the package into the outgoing bin with a hundred other similar items encased in brown.

G.T. guided his crew back outside onto the sidewalk where Chrissie and Melissa skipped ahead as their final destination came into view. Once they were out of hearing range, Claire turned to G.T. "You shouldn't have made such a big production of that,

G.T. They're bound to be doubly disappointed when it comes back rejected now."

"Do you think so?" he inquired as he took her hand and swung it idly between them.

She wondered if he was aware of what he was doing. She, for one, was extremely cognizant of the physical contact. Holding her hand as they walked down the street was not a brotherly-in-law thing to do.

"I thought they might enjoy making a big production out of the send-off. And did you see the looks on their faces when I told them the editor's brains had all leaked out and that's why they hadn't bought your books in the past? They were so wonderfully repulsed they could hardly stand it."

The girls were already on the swings when G.T. and Claire turned into the park. Melissa was pumping for all she was worth, but her actions were reversed—she sat up for the forward swings and leaned back for the opposite—so she was going nowhere fast. Chrissie wasn't even trying. She had taken to the swing on her belly and pushed herself with a running ground stride.

"It was great fun," Claire admitted as she watched the joys of her life at play. She probably wouldn't have taken the time to bring them here if G.T. hadn't stopped by. He'd turned the whole afternoon into a lighthearted celebration. "But I still think it's going to be that much harder now when the put-down comes."

G.T. surprised her.

"I thought of that," he said. "And I've got it covered or I never would have made such a production out of it. I've got a friend who's into bookbinding," he told her.

"You do?"

"Yes. And if by some chance the editor's brains really have leaked out and they don't buy your book, I'll have my friend make two copies up for me and I'd like to give them to the girls for Christmas. In fact, I was thinking of maybe a Toaster and Maureen anthology kind of thing. You know, a collection of all the stories you've written that they could have, keep and maybe read to their own children someday."

Claire was unbearably touched. In fact, her eyes came dangerously close to overflowing. "That would really be nice," she managed to say.

"I try," he responded as he stopped by the park bench.

That was something she was learning about him. Something she didn't want to learn.

He swung the pack with the juice boxes and cookies off his back and set it on the park bench. "Guard this," he instructed. "I can see I've got my work cut out for me teaching those two how to pump."

Claire looked at him thoughtfully. "You know, I don't think I've ever seen a policeman wearing a backpack before."

"Yeah, well, I'm not sure the chief has, either, so let's just keep it between you and me, all right?" he asked as he strode off, leaving Claire to work on the puzzle that was G.T.

Chapter Five

Claire watched G.T. patiently instructing Melissa in the art of pumping while at the same time pushing Chrissie. When she tired of trying to fathom the male mind, she got up and wandered over to the swing set.

"Boy, Missy, it's a good thing this swing's poles are set in concrete. Otherwise, with the way you've been pumping, I suspect you'd be halfway to the moon about now."

Melissa's eyes lit at that. "Wouldn't that be the best ever? I'd be just like an astronaut then."

Claire laughed. "I guess I'll have to be grateful for the concrete then, won't I, lamb chop? I'd miss you if you pumped your way into outer space."

"I wouldn't," Chrissie chipped in. "If Missy went to the moon, I'd have Mommy *and* the cookies we made all to myself."

"You're mean," Melissa shot back.

Before Claire could do anything to turn the conversation from its downward spiral, G.T. stepped in.

"Okay, time's up," he said.

The girls looked at him in surprise. "What time?" Melissa asked.

"Why, your time on the swings, of course. Don't you remember?" He appeared amazed at their forgetfulness. "Tell you what, I'll make a deal with you." He studied his wrist. "You've had fourteen minutes, twenty-nine—and a half seconds. Now if you and Chrissie go sit on the bench and, without arguing," he hastened to stipulate, "drink your juice and eat your cookies while your mom and I take our turns swinging, we'll push you when it's your turn again."

Missy was prepared to argue. "But I can pump—"

G.T. held up a cautionary hand. "*And,* if it's all right with your mother, we'll stop for burgers and fries on the way home. How's that?"

"Deal," Melissa agreed promptly. Come on, Chrissie, let's go. Race you. Ready, set go!" Melissa took off.

"No fair!" Chrissie shrieked as she tore after her sister. "You're supposed to give me a head start 'cuz your legs are longer."

G.T. turned to Claire and grinned lopsidedly. "Well, it was worth a try."

He was going to have to stop smiling like that, Claire decided then and there. At least around her. G.T.'s grin did funny things to her equilibrium. She lowered herself onto the swing and began to pump. Maybe the soft breeze she generated would revive her senses.

G.T. sat with a sigh of relief. He adjusted his gun and night stick so they wouldn't dig into his side. He too began to pump slowly, oblivious to the effect a cop in full paraphernalia playing in the park might have on any passersby. Claire couldn't imagine her ex-husband being that secure. She swung silently for a moment, letting her feet drag a bit in the worn patch of dirt directly under the swing. A small cloud of dust rose.

"Want to see me go around the world?"

The swing set began to shake as G.T. went higher and higher. "Don't you dare," she hissed. "The girls could get hurt if they see you and then try it themselves. It's bad ex—"

A shriek pierced the air. "Uncle G.T., come quick! It's a bee! It's after my juice. What if he stings me?"

Claire jumped mid-swing and ran towards her offspring. "A bee. I knew they'd find that juice. Stay calm, Chrissie. Stop running around and don't panic. I just knew this was going to happen. Hold still Melissa. All that jumping around is going to excite him even more."

And besides, G.T. thought as he brought his trip around the world to a neck snapping stop and followed at a slower pace, Claire was doing enough jumping around for all three of them. "Claire, calm down. Killer bees haven't gotten this far north."

"Oh, if that isn't just like a man—"

Melissa was good and agitated by then. "Bees talk to each other," she said. "I saw it on TV. They do bee dances and buzz around their hive and then the other bees know just where to go. He's getting filled up right now on our juice and then he's going to go tell all the other bees right where we are."

"He's not going anywhere," G.T. assured him as he reached the park bench. "I've got him covered." He waved the bee off with his hand. It circled the bench once or twice, then zeroed back in on the juice box.

"Oh, that was certainly effective," Claire said sardonically. She was feeling much better now that her progeny had been removed to a safe distance.

"Under arrest him," Chrissie yelled. "He wrecked all our fun."

"Yes, G.T.," Claire encouraged. "Take the bee down to the station and throw the book at him."

G.T. took another swipe at the determined insect. "Quiet," he growled.

"Look," Melissa called as she pointed. "He's practicin' his dance, gettin' ready to go home and bring all his bee friends back."

G.T. turned his back to them before he rolled his eyes. Then he took of his uniform cap and eyed it carefully. If he smacked the little yellow and black marauder with his good hat, it would be covered with bee guts as well as become misshapen. That left his bare hand. He sighed and took care of the job. "Damn it."

"What? Did you miss?"

"No, I didn't miss. Let's just say the little bugger didn't go down without a fight."

"He bit you? Oh, G.T., I'm so sorry. Here, let's soak it in the drinking fountain. Maybe the water will still be cold enough to do some good."

The sting was uncomfortable, but not unbearably so. Still he allowed Claire to fuss. Her hands on his were cool and gentle as she gravely inspected the sting mark. He bore it all stoically and everyone was most impressed with his bravery. He decided that saving them from the tiny bandit had been most worthwhile.

When they finally left the park, the shadows cast by the trees bordering the area had swallowed the park. The warmth of the September afternoon was unwillingly surrendering to the cool of a late summer evening. They turned into the hamburger joint and Claire, without ever having issued an invitation, found herself preparing to share her small family's evening meal with G.T.

"So, what do you want on your burger?" he asked as he fished his wallet out of his rear pocket.

"G.T., you don't need to treat us," Claire said. "In fact, after what you've been through, I should be paying for you as well."

"Don't be silly. We civil servants don't make much serving the public duty, but it's enough to pay for a round of hamburgers and fries."

Claire felt as though she'd spent the last several days losing these small skirmishes with her old brother-in-law, but somehow she couldn't summon up the strength to argue with him. Some courtroom lawyer she'd make, she thought in disgust as she threw up her hands in defeat. "So fine, pay for the whole thing, be my guest."

"That's what I like best about you, Claire. Gracious, even in defeat."

"Oh, go sit on a tack." And she hoped he never figured out her verbal sparring was simply a defense against the weakness she felt in her knees every time he showed up.

"May I take your order?"

It was their turn, and G.T. turned to the man behind the counter who hovered over his cash register, his finger poised over the buttons. The guy was ready.

"Four double cheeseburgers, four medium fries—"

Claire hastily interrupted. "That's too much food. The girls can split a double cheeseburger and—"

"Mom?"

"What?

"Can we have some pop, too? Please? Our bones won't turn to sponges, we promise."

Claire steeled herself to their pleading faces. "No. You know soda's not good for growing bodies. We've got a whole gallon of milk at home. We can have that."

"Two large and two small colas."

Claire swung around, her eyes wide. "G.T.!"

"And four hot apple pies. That's it. Oh, to go."

"Right, that's four double cheese, four medium fries, two large, two small colas and four apple pies. Eleven dollars and ninety-seven cents, please."

G.T. handed over a ten and two singles and the clerk dribbled the three pennies into his hand in return. Absently he turned them over in his hand, checking their dates and condition. "Did you know the United States has never minted a penny for use here in this country?" he asked as he turned to her.

She recognized the old subject change as avoidance mechanism when she saw it. She'd used it herself many a time. However, he had spiked her interest and she went for the bait. "Oh? Then what're those in your hand?" She nodded at the shiny copper in his palm.

"A lot of nothing more than face-value garbage, near as I can tell," he grumbled, sliding the three pennies into his pocket. "Nothing worth keeping. But seriously, those are not pennies, they're one-cent coins. The term "penny" is nothing but a holdover from our old English roots."

"What's that supposed to mean?" she asked suspiciously as she watched their order taker capping off the four unwanted drinks.

"England has a coin called a penny. It's a percentage of their pound. Because of our English heritage, though, people started calling our one-cent coins pennies and it stuck. Isn't that interesting?"

"Sort of," she grudgingly admitted. "But about those sodas—"

"Claire, be serious," he instructed.

As though she'd ever been allowed to be anything but, she thought a bit resentfully.

"They're going to die from a heart attack as a result of all the cholesterol in the hamburger and French fries long before their bones decalcify from drinking the pop. Face it, there's no salvaging this meal and no putting a good face on it."

"I was going to make vegetables when we got home," she protested. "Green beans, as a matter of fact."

"Okay, let's go do it," he agreed as he accepted the white bag from the man whose name tag read George. "I promise I'll eat my share, but I need the pop." He crossed his fingers behind his back. "I hear it's very good for counteracting the venom from bee bites."

"That's meat tenderizer, you twerp, and you very well know it."

He shrugged. "So we'll try both when we get to your place."

And that was how Claire found herself with four around her kitchen table once more. She served green beans and opened a can of fruit cocktail to go with the fast food and she made everyone drink a glass of milk to counteract the soda pop.

"The fat in the milk is only going to coat our arteries," G.T. warned as he chugged it down.

"It's skim," she informed him smugly. "All the bad stuff has been taken out."

"Ugh, I can tell," he said as he came up for air. "This tastes like water."

"When you're an old man bent over with osteoporosis while I am still perfectly upright and riding the swings with my grandchildren, I will take great pleasure in saying, 'Ha ha, told you so.'"

And he had no doubt she would, too. "That would be very small of you," he felt obliged to mention.

She swept hamburger wrappers off the table and into the trash. She refused to feel guilty. Hadn't G.T. spent the whole afternoon overruling her maternal authority? She might have to wait for forty years to get her revenge, but, hey, small people learned early in life to take it when they could. "It will be not only fulfilling, but also a whole lot of fun."

G.T. rose with the ketchup in hand and returned it to the refrigerator. "You're heartless."

Her posture straightened at that. "Why, thank you." She just might make a good lawyer yet.

He shook his head. "That wasn't a compliment," he informed her as the doorbell rang.

"I wonder who that could be," Claire asked in surprise. "I'm not expecting anybody."

"I'll get it," Missy offered and took off for the front hall.

"Don't you open that door without putting the chain on it first," G.T. yelled after her.

"It's probably just a neighbor needing to borrow something," Claire soothed. "But if you're that worried, why don't you go answer it? Any bad guys will take one look at your badge and all that hardware you're carting around on your belt and take off in the opposite direction."

"I'll darn well see that they do," he shot back before stalking down the hall after the girls. What was wrong with that woman anyway? If he sounded the slightest bit protective she got so darned prickly. He knew she needed to prove her independence, but he couldn't help worrying about her and the girls. *Some* women like having a guy like him watching over them. Problem was, he didn't give a hoot about any woman but Claire.

The little girls were still working on the front door lock when he reached it and G.T. realized siblings born that close together would probably argue about anything.

"It goes this way, dumb bunny."

"No, it don't. And I'm gonna tell Mommy you called me a bad name."

Gently, G.T. eased the quarreling twosome to one side. "It's all right, girls. I'm here now." He opened the door. "Yes?"

"A policeman, oh thank God! How did Claire know?"

This is what came from being in a hurry. Police uniforms attracted crazies like, well, like apple juice attracted bees. He should have taken the time to change. Even the city's servants deserved some time to themselves. Now he was stuck dealing with this—person who had combined an obviously expensive silk business dress with fuzzy pink mule slippers. He rolled his eyes before he could stop himself. "Is there a problem, ma'am?"

An expression of horror rolled over the woman's features. "You're not here because of Claire, are you?"

While G.T. pondered the answer to that—*was* he there because of Claire?—the woman clarified the question.

"I mean, the burglars didn't come here, too?"

Whoa. Burglars? "What burglars?" he questioned carefully, not liking the sound of this at all.

"I just got home from work," the woman told him excitedly. "I stepped inside my front door. My feet were killing me, so first thing I put down my briefcase, kicked off my high heels and slipped on my scuffs."

G.T. almost rolled his eyes again, but managed to stop in the nick of time. "Claire, could you come out here for a minute?" he called. He closed the door just long enough to slip the chain off. The woman did not stop talking for an instant.

"Then I looked around. Sometimes the cat gets mad when I leave and he knocks over the plants, you know? So I was checking to see if there were any major cleanups waiting for me, and what do you think?" the unknown woman asked, hands windmilling expressively in front of her.

"Claire?"

"The whole place was totaled. The cat's never been that mad. I've been robbed, I know it! I was too scared to stay there alone and wanted to use the phone to call the police, but here you are. Now you come with me and I'll show you—"

Before G.T. could reply, Claire appeared at his side, and the neighbor began telling her story all over again.

"Someone's been in my apartment," the woman announced starkly. "They may still be there, for all I know. As soon as I came in the front door and glanced around, I backed right out again."

"That's terrible! You come right in here and stay with the girls while G.T. and I check your apartment over."

G.T. thought about it in plenty of time, then rolled his eyes anyway. Like he would almost let Claire do an apartment sweep with him. Unfortunately, he knew better than to assume she'd stay put should he go off on his own to check things out. "Uncle G.T.'s got a great idea, kiddies. Let's call 911. You can practice just the way Officer Friendly taught you."

"Why should we bother the people at 911 when you and I are right here?" Claire asked practically. "Come on, G.T., it'll be fun."

Fun? Had she said *fun?* It was all he could do to keep his mouth from hanging open. Is that what she thought he did all day? Partied from one crime scene to the next? "Claire," he explained carefully, "sweeping a crime scene is not exactly the equivalent of going on a picnic."

"I know that," Claire said as she pulled Wynetta in from the hall. "So fun wasn't the right word. It would be exciting."

Exciting and perhaps—daring? G.T. narrowed his eyes as he considered the wide-eyed innocent in front of him. Claire breaking a bit more of the shell she'd been living in? One of these days he'd convince her it wasn't necessary to use a sledge hammer. "Listen, I can see that Wynetta's upset, and I'm willing to go check things out, but I'm going alone. And that's final." Claire's presence would not only violate half a dozen police procedures rules, she'd also be far too distracting. Besides, he'd give her all the excitement she could possibly crave later on, when they'd gotten rid of Wynetta and the girls were in bed for the night. Oh, man, where had that come from? He'd probably be killed in there. All it took were *thoughts* of Claire and he was distracted.

"Oh, all right," Claire caved in reluctantly. She gazed after G.T. as he started down the hall.

"You be careful."

He could almost hear her gnawing her lip. Why was he out here in the hall when he could be in there soothing that hurt with his own mouth? "That does it," he muttered, appalled by the direction of his thoughts. "I'll make sure the joker's cleared out, then I'm out of here myself. I should never have tried to go around the world on the swing set. Not only did Claire get mad at me for swinging too high, but I think I rattled my brains, as well."

"G.T., wait!" Claire called after him.

He sighed and halted in his tracks. "Now what?"

"I'm going to call the police. You should have some back up."

"Good idea. You do that." With all the ruckus they'd raised, any burglar worth his crowbar would be long gone. The only way he'd still be around was if he'd been forced into a life of crime in order to pay for a hearing aid.

He found Wynetta's apartment. It was the only one with the door hanging open. He backed up to the adjacent wall as he approached it and drew his gun.

He slid sideways through the doorway and let his eyes sweep the room. Wynetta was right. He doubted any cat, no matter how vindictive it was feeling, could have done this. Over the furniture cushions, lamps and debris tossed in the middle of the room, he could see two doorways off the living room. He hated it when that happened. Whichever one he checked first, he'd have his back to the other when he went in. He stuck to the perimeter of the room and edged his way to one of the doors. Again he slid sideways, shifting his vision back and forth between the room he was entering and the one he was leaving.

"Gotta be Wynetta's bedroom." He pegged the room immediately even though the mattress had been dumped on the floor and the closet emptied. Evidently Wynetta had a thing for slippers. Several pairs lay strewn about, including one with high heels edged in fake fur. "Man, oh, man. How'd she ever fit all this stuff in the closet in the first place?" Was this all standard female paraphernalia? Did Claire have silk brassieres and panties like that? He wouldn't mind seeing her in the peach set hanging off the end of the bed. He swallowed hard, then forced himself to methodically check any possible hiding places, never leaving his back to the door. Nobody in the bedroom except himself, not even the cat. That left whatever was behind the other opening in the living room. Had to be the kitchen. Gun still in hand, he began to sidle back out into the living room.

"G.T.? G.T.? You in here?"

He swung around, leveling his gun as he pivoted.

Claire entered the apartment and found herself face-to-face with his revolver.

"Claire! My God, what are you doing here? I told you to stay locked in your apartment until I made sure it was safe. What is the matter with you, woman? I could have killed you!"

"No, you wouldn't have. That's why I made all the noise coming in—so you'd know it was me and not the bad guy. You were gone so long I got worried about you. I just wanted to check that you were all right."

He stared at her in amazement for a good long moment.

"Do you think you could point that thing someplace else?" Claire finally requested. "I didn't make this mess, honest."

Maybe not this one, but she was doing a pretty thorough job on his heart. He spoke slowly, each word succinct and drawn out. "Get out of here and do not come back until I give the all clear. You are to go back to your apartment and keep the door closed and locked *with* the chain on until I tell you otherwise. Got that?"

She made a helpless gesture with her hands. "Wynetta locked herself in with the kids when I came. I'm not sure she'll let me back in without you there to give the all clear."

Briefly he closed his eyes. It was one thing for Claire to dye her hair and whack it off. It might take a while, but she could always grow it back. Even going to law school qualified as a misguided but relatively harmless way of working out her current need to appear decisive and an independent thinker. But this was unforgivable. Stubborn, dumb, dangerous. She needed to be taken in hand, and just as soon as he was done here—done here? He opened his eyes. "Stay right where you are," he directed. "Don't move, don't even *twitch* until I'm back. You hear?"

Her eyes opened wide at his tone. Well, too damn bad. She nodded her agreement, and that was the important part. Honestly, how was he supposed to take care of her and keep her safe if she insisted on waltzing gaily into disaster? He gave her one last hard look to make sure she was staying put, then slipped into what did indeed turn out to be the kitchen. A breeze moved through the room and G.T. identified its source as the back door. It squeaked gently on its hinges as it reacted to the evening air currents.

Immediately a sense of relief flowed over him. He checked the pantry and broom closet, anyway, but that only verified what he already knew. The thief was gone. He heard voices in the hallway and knew the police had arrived. "As soon as I explain the situation to them, I'll take Claire back to the apartment, send Wynetta back here to make a statement and murder Claire in peace."

He strode out into the living room. "I'll really give her a piece of my mind I can barely afford," he promised himself as he holstered his gun.

He found Claire explaining the situation to the officer in charge. "He's long gone," he told his colleague. Shortly thereafter, he promised to send Wynetta back—provided he could get her to unlock Claire's door—and ushered Claire out of there.

It took a while, but eventually he had Claire to himself and found himself in the position of needing to yell, but having to do it quietly, so as not to wake the girls. He sat her on the sofa while he sat right on the edge of the wingback next to it, his posture rigid as he expounded on the stupidity of blithely walking into a situation such as that. He didn't even think to question the depth of his ire.

"I just wanted to make sure you hadn't been hurt in there."

"Never, never, *never* do anything like that again."

Claire was the picture of innocence. "I don't see why you're so upset. It was really all your fault."

"My fault!" He became even more incensed when she did not appear properly contrite.

She nodded. "Absolutely. You should have checked in with us from time to time. You were gone so long, anybody would have been worried."

G.T. hung on to his temper—barely. "It takes time to sweep a crime scene, Claire," he explained with exaggerated patience. "What if I had sent your friend back into an apartment and the perpetrator was still hiding in her closet? She could have been hurt or worse."

Claire sat back. "Oh. I hadn't thought of that."

"I realize this isn't your line of work, but it is mine. You should have followed my instructions."

"But if you *had* been hurt—"

"You'd already called 911, right? They'd have taken care of me."

She looked ready to argue some more and he sighed. "Do you have any idea what it would have done to those two little girls in there if you'd been hurt? To me?" The question surprised him. Well, heck, who wouldn't be upset if a beautiful young woman was hurt? Nobody, that's who. His concern was perfectly normal. Absolutely and completely.

Claire looked a bit forlorn as she sat on the sofa fidgeting with a pearl ring she wore. The adrenaline that had carried G.T. through the past few hours drained out of his system, leaving him feeling deflated. He moved over to the sofa and sat next to her. Next thing he knew, he'd taken her hand in his. "Claire, honey—"

She looked up and he was caught in those oddly vulnerable blue eyes. Her shoulders began to tremble slightly and the oversize garish hoops in her earlobes began to swing. He couldn't stand it. He slid his arm around her and pulled her close. Without conscious decision, he found his mouth touching hers. All hell broke loose as every nerve ending in his body responded to the perceived emergency. Damn, he really hated this, he thought just before deepening the kiss.

Chapter Six

The woman was lethal, he thought hazily as he pulled her closer. If he could just regain control of his careering senses long enough to put a coherent thought together, he was sure he could come up with some kind of arrestable offense heading that what she was doing to him would fall under. Unfortunately that wasn't too likely anytime in the near future.

Claire, who'd initially been somewhat stiff in his arms, was now melting all over him. He could smell her subtle perfume. All the polished moves he'd worked on perfecting for years—since the onset of puberty—deserted him now. He groaned at the injustice of it all. God, how he hated feeling unsure of himself, and Claire did that to him.

He collapsed against the sofa back and Claire followed him down. He combed her hair with his fingers and wished he'd had the opportunity to try it when she'd had shoulder length tresses. Then again, her shorter cut certainly made it easy to trace the delicate contour of her ear and the graceful line of her neck. Her earrings of the day consisted of large red circlets with green and yellow parrots clinging precariously to the inside of the hoop. He touched one and watched Polly sway on her perch. They enchanted him. *She* enchanted him. He leaned to kiss her lobe.

"G.T.?"

"Yeah?" he growled.

"We shouldn't be doing this." Her voice came out low and thready.

He loved that, even though she was right. Of course they shouldn't be doing this. Every self-protective instinct he had was screaming at him. And he was intent on ignoring them all. She was undoubtedly right. His instincts were undoubtedly right. But weren't you supposed to learn from your mistakes? They should think of this as a learning experience, he decided. And he was ready for some serious advancement in his studies.

G.T. touched his lips to her temple, then her collarbone. "We'll stop," he promised. "In a little while." He moved his mouth to her brow.

Claire felt the touch of his lips and the accompanying small jolt made her jump. She didn't understand any of this. She'd never felt anything so intensely. Never ever. She looped her hands behind his head and tugged his face towards her. She wanted to feel that buzz again, only more intimately. Claire met his mouth with hers and the sensation stunned her. "How do you *do* that?" she asked when G.T. finally broke the contact.

"It's not me," he told her seriously. "I have to confess, I've done my share of kissing since I turned eleven—"

She leaned back and looked at him. "Eleven?"

He reddened. "Yeah, well Mary Sue Berbinsky developed pretty early. Fifth grade, and she was already like this." He made a gesture with his hands two feet out in front of his chest.

"Good grief."

He traced her arched brows and then the lines of her disapproving pout. "But like I was saying, it's not me. In all those years I've never felt anything like this. It's got to be you."

"It's new to me, too," she protested, already sinking under the spell of his hypnotizing finger. "It's almost like there's an electrical short somewhere and the sofa's not grounded." But she wasn't about to get up and off that sofa, not for a million dollars.

G.T. smiled seductively. "If it's not either one of us, then it must be something special that only happens when we're with each other and it doesn't work with anybody else." Scary thought, but hey, policemen were supposed to like living on the edge. He looked down into the luminous eyes a scant few inches from his own and knew it was true.

She glossed over her lips with the tip of her tongue and then closed the gap between them.

G.T. was just sure she'd wet her lips to see if she could improve the contact. It had worked. His nerve pathways practically hummed as Claire rubbed his mouth with hers. If he never got any closer to heaven than this, it would be all right, he decided.

"This is stupid," Claire murmured, but she obligingly threw her head back to allow G.T.'s lips easier access to her throat.

"Yes," he agreed as he approached her collarbone.

"Don't stop," she instructed.

"No." Thank God for her honesty. Stopping would probably half kill him at this point.

The neckline of her shirt was too constricted to suit his need and Claire gasped when he pulled the blouse free of her waistband. G.T. watched her eyes drift shut and the tip of her tongue catch her upper lip when he slipped his hands under the knit fabric and ran them up her ribs. His thumbs took the weight of her small breasts and he felt her breath catch for a moment. It pleased him that his touch could make her do that. Turnabout was fair play, after all and her butterfly caresses had him about ready to go off like the scoreboard at Comiskey Park after a White Sox home run.

He massaged her breasts and let his thumbs circle her nipples through the thin cotton of her brassiere. G.T. was aware of air catching in her lungs again. His relationship with Claire was metamorphosing with every second they spent on her sofa. He had no idea any more if that was good or bad. It just was, ready or not. He debated if he should release the catch on her bra or divest himself of the gun, walkie-talkie, handcuffs and other assorted appurtenances currently poking him in the back and side.

He slid one hand around to her back and reached for his belt buckle with the other.

Claire jerked upright, stymieing his one-handed attempts at loosening her bra. "What was that?"

"What was what?"

"That noise. Didn't you hear it?" She cocked her head. "There it is again. Listen."

He hadn't heard anything. Frankly, an earthquake could have struck and the apartment up above could have come crashing down on top of them and he doubt he'd have heard it. "What'd it sound like?" he asked, disgusted with the amount of time it was taking him to clear his head.

She snapped her fingers. "There!" Then she sagged against the sofa back and pushed her wispy bangs back off her forehead. "Never mind," she muttered. "I know what it is. One of the boards holding Melissa's spring and mattress in the frame creaks when she turns over. That's what it was."

"Oh." G.T. sat up and put his head into his hands. Rubbing his eyes, he contemplated the situation. It was a new one for him. Was he supposed to ignore the interruption and carry on, so to speak, or had the mood been broken? Women were touchy about things like that. And he was forced to admit that Claire was more woman than he'd ever known.

"G.T.?"

He twisted his head in his palms and glanced over at her. Her hands were knotted together and she seemed to be struggling to untwist them. He knew he had the answer to his question. "Yeah, honey?"

"Things are going pretty quickly here, don't you think? You and I—"

"Barely know each other?" he finished with a wry grimace.

"Well of course we *know* each other, just not in this particular way, if you know what I mean," she finished lamely but determinedly. "And I just think that at this point in my life, when I'm supposed to be learning to stand on my own two feet—that is the point of my going back to school, after all—that it's a mistake to get involved with somebody like you."

"Somebody like me?" he echoed carefully. What was that supposed to mean? What was he, King Kong? Did she think he was going to kidnap her and cart her up to the top of the Empire State Building? By God, remarks like that combined with all the grief she'd given him that afternoon were enough to make him try it. Only he'd drop her off the roof once he got her up there!

Self-consciously, she tucked her blouse back in. "I didn't mean it in a bad way, but you have to admit you're rather overprotective of the girls and me."

He didn't have to admit any such thing. "Asking you to keep out of a potentially dangerous crime scene and to use the safety chain on your door is not overprotectiveness," he informed her, feeling rather put upon, "it is simple common sense."

Claire brushed her bangs back again. "I'm not explaining this very well."

He stood, shoving the end of his belt back into place. He shouldn't be feeling irritated. He should be grateful, extremely grateful, in fact. She was giving them time to think this through, keeping them from making a potentially serious error here. Was *he* ready to take this next step?

Unfortunately, he didn't feel the least bit grateful to her for her cold feet. He was ticked as hell. Overprotective, hah!

What he knew was that he needed to go home and go to bed. Get some sleep. Bee venom was affecting his brain. Maybe a restorative night's sleep would bring back some sense of perspective. He was all set to announce his imminent departure, in fact, when a terrible thought hit him.

What if the creep who'd struck Wynetta's place came back? It wasn't unheard of for a burglar who'd found an easy building to come back and strike the same place again, sometimes several times.

"I'm staying the night," he announced as he thought the situation through.

"No you're not. I told you, I'm not sure I'm ready for anything like this between us."

He dismissed her concerns with a flick of his hand. He had more important things on his mind now, although he doubted *she'd* understand that. He'd give her overprotective. Her safety transcended mere sex and if that wasn't a noble sentiment on his part, he didn't know what would qualify. "I'm not talking about *that*. I understand the word *no*. I—"

"I just think—"

He had no time right then to plumb the depths of her feminine mind. He'd been trying to get a fix on that elusive free-floating organ for years. His inability to do so was a good part of the reason he'd reached the age of twenty-eight with his bachelorhood still intact. "We can clear up the semantics of your putting the kibosh on things tonight some other time. For now, let me make it clear that while I do intend to stay the night—no, let me finish—I'll be sleeping on the sofa."

"But, G.T., why?" Claire asked helplessly. "I'm not going to change my mind, if that's what you're thinking, not tonight at any rate."

"Would you stop with the sex stuff? I am not pressuring you, so kindly stop acting as though I was. Man, I thought it was *men* that were supposed to have the one-track minds." He stood and eyed the sofa with disfavor. The only appealing thing about it was Claire huddled there in the middle, staring up at him with her beguilingly wide blue eyes. And he was beguiled for some reason tonight. He shook his head and freed himself from her spell. He'd get over it. He'd always gotten over infatuations in the past. Staying overnight tonight was a job, nothing more, nothing less. Professionalism, there was the key. "I want to be here in case the guy who rifled your neighbor's place decides this building is easy pickings and comes back. I don't want him walking in on you while you're asleep."

He could only imagine the vision she'd present. The guy would have to be a candidate for sainthood—which wasn't likely if he was burglarizing the place—to pass up the opportunities a sight like that would present. Heck, G.T. was a certified hero—he had the citation to prove it—and *he* was going to have a hell of a time passing it up. Probably wouldn't get any sleep at all.

Claire, who'd been halfway up out of the sofa, sank back down. "You think that's likely?"

He didn't want to unduly scare her, but he didn't want her blowing his concern off, either. "It's been known to happen," he allowed carefully.

"Frequently?"

"Ah, I don't have exact percentages. And what does it matter? If he comes back tonight he's not going to find a defenseless single woman, is he?"

Her eyes narrowed at what she perceived as a slur. "No, he'll find the rough, tough, macho cop who faces down bees with nothing but his bare hands, won't he? I'm surprised you didn't take out your gun and shoot the poor little thing."

He rolled his eyes.

"I saw that," she snapped.

"I can't help it, it's genetic."

"Oh, yeah, right. Genetic."

He sighed, but managed not to roll. "I believe we may be getting off the track here. I—"

She snapped her fingers. "I know. You could leave me your gun. Or your nightstick. I could keep it under my pillow and you could pick it up in the morning on your way to work."

He was instantly appalled. "Claire! Don't you even think about keeping a weapon in this house. The odds are extremely high it would be wrestled away and used against you. And a gun! You aren't trained to handle it, and even if you were, guess who's the most likely victim?"

She stood, nibbling a fingertip as she began to pace the length of the small room. "Oh, yeah. Right. Forget I said that. That was really stupid of me. I wouldn't want the girls to find it and hurt themselves."

Claire still had that finger in her mouth as she approached him. What he wouldn't give to nibble it for her. She took it out and pointed it at him. It glistened moistly in the light thrown by the lamp on the end table next to the sofa. He stared at the finger. Men had suffered heart failure from less, he was sure.

"You know what? Tomorrow I'll start going through the yellow pages. I just wasn't thinking properly. Of course I don't want any weapons in the house. What I need to do is learn some self-defense. Maybe

I'll earn a black belt in something. What do you think? Is karate or tae kwon do better?"

He exerted extreme control and barely managed to keep his eyes straight. If he wasn't very careful here, his eyeball muscles were going to short out from all the strain he was putting on them. Then his eyes would probably roll all the way to the back of his head. Just his luck they'd get stuck there, too. But did she really think he'd let some unknown goon who'd probably been thrown on his head once too often learning his trade teach her self-defense? Touch her in any way whatsoever?

Unfortunately, there was no logical reason for her not to do this. Rationally speaking, it was actually a rather good idea. One out of every three women would be a crime victim at some point in their life. They *should* know some self-defense techniques. Too bad he wasn't operating rationally just then. "I'll teach you myself." He heard the words come out of his mouth and knew as they spilled into the room between them they'd get him into trouble. Hadn't he just promised to behave? Hadn't he? And now here he'd just arranged things so he'd be *touching* her, maybe not intimately, but still his hands would be on her while he showed her the moves she'd need to know. He'd never thought of himself as a martyr before, but he was beginning to suspect he might have a latent self-preservation problem, after all.

Claire shook her head as she stood there in front of him. "That's all right, G.T. It'd be better if I call around, I think."

Damn it, why didn't she stop all her infernal thinking? He'd never met anyone whose mere thought processes could be so completely annoying. Women!

The Lord had been on a roll for a while there. Why hadn't he quit while he was ahead? "Claire, I will teach you whatever you need to know about self-defense, all right? All right."

She put her hands on her hips and got right up into his face. Him, a cop twice her size and in full uniform, and here was this wild woman in his face.

"I don't want to be unkind, G.T., but, I mean, this is important to me. So, uh, do you have any qualifications for this?"

He was so taken aback, his mouth actually fell open. "Qualifications?" Had the hair dye gone through to her brain? "Claire, I'm a policeman, in case you hadn't noticed."

"Of course I noticed," she returned with exaggerated patience. "I also noticed your gun, handcuffs, two-way radio, nightstick and flashlight. I won't have any of those props, remember? Just me and my bare hands. Oh, and my wits."

G.T. threw up his hands. Well, the whole thing was a loss, then because he'd just about decided she didn't have any of those. The Biblical Samson had lost his strength when he'd had his hair cut. Maybe Claire had lost her wits, who could tell? "For your information, the police department runs self-defense clinics for women a couple of times a year. I've taught it myself once or twice."

She looked doubtful. "You have? You can teach me how to throw somebody who grabs me from behind?"

"If somebody jumps you, honey, you don't want to get fancy. Just get him off balance long enough to break his hold, then run like hell."

"I want to learn to throw somebody. It would be fun to flip some jerk over my shoulder and stomp him into the pavement, I think."

A newly liberated woman was a dangerous thing, he discovered then and there. He decided the better part of valor would be to simply terminate the discussion, so he went over to the lamp on the end table and twisted the switch. Instantly the room darkened.

"Why'd you do that?"

"I don't know about you, but I need some sleep. My shift starts at seven and you've got those two little girls to cope with bright and early in the morning. How about if we deal with the question of flipping bad guys another time?"

"But—"

"Please?"

It struck her as so incongruous for this gun-toting, overly large macho male to be pleading to go to bed that she agreed. "All right," she said.

She retrieved a pillow and sheet from the small closet in the hall and handed them to him. In the quiet, dark room, the gesture seemed intimate somehow, even though his hand didn't linger when he took the linens. "Well, I'll see you in the morning, then."

"Right," he said, already involved in spreading the sheet. "The morning."

She hovered uncertainly in the doorway for a moment, not quite sure how to handle the peculiar situation. She watched G.T. remove his belt and all its attendant hardware. "I guess I'll say good-night," she finally said.

"Good night," he mumbled in return, then sank gratefully into the sofa, turning his back to the room.

HARDHEADED WOMAN

She guessed she'd been dismissed, so she left, oddly disappointed that he hadn't even attempted to kiss her good-night.

She checked on the girls and dawdled in the bathroom, convinced she wouldn't sleep at all. And, in fact, when she ran out of reasons to procrastinate and flipped the covers back on her queen-size bed, for the first time in months it felt lonely in there. Which didn't mean that if he was to show up in the doorway right then she wouldn't argue with him. She would. She just didn't know how sincere her side of the argument would be or, for that matter, who'd win.

She stared up at the ceiling for several minutes while she pondered that, but fell solidly asleep before she'd reached any kind of conclusion.

The morning light surprised her. Since the first night she'd been on her own with just the girls for company, she'd *always* started awake at least once during the night. Either there'd been a dearth of the odd kinds of noises this apartment building specialized in last night, or she'd felt secure enough with G.T. out there on the sofa that she'd allowed herself to really sink into a deep slumber.

She squinted at the clock on the nightstand. "Look at that," she muttered. "It's seven o'clock already. I slept right through." She stretched. It felt great. With a sense of anticipation she left her bed and went out to the living room.

The couch was empty.

Down at the end of the hall, the bathroom door hung open and the kitchen was silent.

He was gone.

"Huh," she grunted. "How about that? I even slept through that." Funnily enough, since she'd argued against his staying at all, she felt deflated now that he'd left. "He could have at least said goodbye," she decided, then spotted the note on the coffee table.

"Dear Claire," she read. *"It's five-thirty and I've got to get going. The sergeant isn't going to appreciate it if I show up looking like I've slept in my uniform. Try—"* She snorted inelegantly to herself at the way he'd underlined the word. *"Try and be good. Give each of the girls a hug from me and I'll see you tonight out at Oakley."*

He'd signed it *"XOXOXOXO, G.T."*

She stared at the boldly slashed *X*s and *O*s. "Look at all those hugs and kisses," she said and was irritated with herself for wanting to experience them a little more personally. "I don't need that kind of stuff anymore," she informed herself stiffly as she crumpled the note in her hand. "And certainly not from another Greer. My life is not a baseball game. Striking out with Arnie was quite enough. I'm under no obligation to give the males in my world another couple of pitches. Forget it.

"I'm an independent woman," she continued as she sailed out of the living room and into the small kitchen. She pulled eggs, milk and bread out of the refrigerator and began preparing French toast. Cracking the eggs into a bowl, she tossed their shells down the garbage disposal and snapped her fingers. "I know what kind of law I'm going to practice. I'll be a divorce lawyer and only take female clients. If there's any question of impropriety at all, even this much—" She stopped whipping the eggs and milk together long enough to hold up her thumb and forefinger. They almost touched. "—I'll take that guy to the cleaners so badly he'll still be smelling the cleaning fluid ten years later."

When she was done frying the bread, the girls were still sleeping, so she set their toast aside, ready to zap when they finally appeared. Meanwhile, she propped up her torts book and once more attempted to make some sense out of it while she tried to convince herself she liked eating breakfast by herself and was *glad*—yes, *glad*—she hadn't woken in time to share it with G.T.

She lifted a forkful of syrupy bread to her mouth and popped it in. Her forehead slowly creased as she chewed while she read. The breeze coming in the window over the sink ruffled the yellow-and-white café curtain she'd hung. The soft snapping of fabric was the only sound in the apartment as she absently took a second bite and tried to concentrate harder.

By her third mouthful, she'd given up and started over. "I can't understand how I had such a high verbal score on my SATs," she finally said, breaking the unnatural silence in the apartment, "when there aren't more than a handful of words on this whole page that I understand. What the heck even *is* a koan?"

She stuffed a piece of French toast in her mouth and went to fetch the dictionary. "It's not even in here," she muttered around the food. Eventually she found a reference in the third source she tried. "A paradox used for meditation, huh? The guy who came up with the word "koan" must have known G.T., if that's what it means." She read further. "Uh-oh, what's this? Buddhist monks use koans to make themselves more open to enlightenment based on intuition instead of being stuck in reason and logic. I thought my ability to reason was what differentiated human beings from the animals. What's going on here?"

Thoughtfully she closed the reference book and returned to her spot at the kitchen table. "Wait'll I tell G.T. this guy is trying to get lawyers to be intuitive rather than rely on reason. He'll flip," she said as she turned on the radio. She kept the volume low, but even that small amount of noise was an improvement. It was just too quiet in the apartment that morning.

She tried once again to concentrate, but it was difficult to understand the judge's reasoning or to even care about some railroadman named Ives who'd been injured back in 1911. The judge's opinion rambled on seemingly forever and frequently referred to seamen and shipowners, for some unknown reason. She polished off the last of her breakfast and rinsed her plate while she thought about poor Ives. "You know what?" she asked of no one in particular as she laid her dish on the drain board. "G.T. would say that this Judge Werner needed to get a life. Anybody who had the time to come up with the sheer amount of convoluted logic this man produced for this case obviously needed more interests in his life. If this is what the halls of law are filled with, it's pathetic. Absolutely no question about it, pathetic." With that pronouncement, she went to wake up the girls. She couldn't tolerate the morning peace and serenity another minute. Not when her insides were so churned up from the day before.

G.T. had basically run yesterday afternoon and evening the way he'd wanted to. He'd contradicted everything she'd said and done it all his way—although, to be fair, he had eaten a healthy portion of the string beans she'd fixed to sort of round out the french fries and greasy burgers they'd bought on the way home from the park.

Imagine a grown man—a grown man in full police uniform—trying to go around the world on the swing. Why, what if the snap closing his gun holster had come undone? His revolver could have fallen out, maybe discharging when it hit the ground. He could have shot himself in the butt, when you stopped and thought about it. And he had a heck of a fine butt, too. He ought to be looking out after that rear instead of purposely putting it into harm's way. Honestly, he was so immature. And pushy. Look at the way he'd pushed her into mailing that manuscript. He hadn't stopped to consider that just maybe she didn't feel like putting herself on the line for another rejection just yet. These things had to be worked up to. Didn't he understand that writing was extremely personal? It was like giving birth, and it hurt like crazy to be told your baby was ugly.

He'd made her do it and now another of her precious offspring waited in a slush pile somewhere in New York to be spurned.

He was a pain in the neck.

And she missed him this morning.

If he had to report at seven, that meant he'd finish up at three. She wondered if he'd stop by. Maybe they could ride out to Oakley together. "Oh, man, I'm going crazy," she moaned as she opened the girls' bedroom door.

Missy stretched and slowly sat up. "What'd you say, Mommy?"

"I said, it's time to get up, sleepyhead." Claire went over and found Chrissie's foot under the sheets. She rubbed it and put a creepy tickle down her leg. "You, too, princess. Rise and shine."

Chrissie opened one eye, then immediately shut it again. "Do we hafta?"

"Yes." On that point, she was clear. It was getting late and she needed more than her own thoughts for company.

Chapter Seven

The day had started off sunny and warm and only improved from there. By ten o'clock it was seventy-five degrees and the sun was so bright, it hurt your eyes. Claire took Chrissie back to the park and sat primly on the park bench, keeping an eye on her while she tried yet one more time to wade through *Ives v. South Buffalo Railroad Co.*

Chrissie left her pretty much alone to contemplate Ives, her toes, and G.T. while she played with the other children in the park.

After struggling for what seemed like hours to get through the first two pages without getting distracted by thoughts of G.T., Claire glanced at her wrist. Ten forty-five. Unbelievable. She sighed, leaned back and took a deep breath. The trees still sported green, healthy looking leaves, but she could smell fall. It was in the air, just biding its time before making an official appearance.

In a few weeks, when the autumn colors came in, she'd see if G.T. wanted to go to the forest preserve with them for a hike. Immediately, she caught herself.

"The girls and I are a complete unit. We don't need G.T.—or anybody else. We'll go by ourselves and have a blast doing it."

The day warmed even further. Must be closing in on eighty degrees, she thought, and glanced again at her wrist. Eleven-ten. Man alive, here it was an absolutely gorgeous day, picture perfect, and it felt as if it would never end.

At eleven-thirty, she and Chrissie started for home, picking up Missy on the way. She gave the girls lunch, read them a story, then settled them in for a nap while she tried yet again to study.

The day wound down from there, dragging its heels and protesting every bit of the way, but eventually the sitter Claire had hired to replace her mother-in-law— what had gotten into that woman? It was so unlike her to take off like that—showed up. G.T. did not. So at a quarter to six she drove herself out to Oakley.

He wasn't in the hallway and he didn't stop by her classroom to check up on her. It was very unlike him. Maybe he'd finally really listened to her and believed she was capable of running her life.

She thought about that.

If that was the case, she wasn't sure she liked it— which just went to show how weird her mind had gone lately. She felt oddly bereft and let down by his lack of concern. Top that.

Then again, he could be hurt. Maybe even in a hospital someplace. Cops got injured in the line of duty all the time; it was possible. Now she felt sick. The professor came in and started shuffling papers in that totally annoying way he had, so she settled stiffly back into her seat and tried to pay attention.

What the heck precinct did G.T. even work in? she asked herself. She should know that.

She couldn't understand the professor's explanation of *Ives* any better than the textbook's. This was seriously depressing. She took notes, writing down everything the man said because she couldn't tell what was important and what wasn't. She'd sort through it later, she decided, and made plans to start calling hospitals on her break.

"Here you are, Claire. I looked all over the cafeteria for you. I bought you an ice-cream bar, but it started to melt, so I ended up having to eat it for you. What are you doing? Calling home to check up on the kids?"

His voice startled her out of her perusal of the yellow pages. She'd been trying to decide which of the hospitals listed on the pages in front of her were on the north side where she knew G.T. practiced his policing. "G.T., it's you! You're all right! Oh, I'm so glad."

He arched a brow. "Yes, it's me, and of course I'm all right. Why wouldn't I be?"

"You didn't call," she accused. "Not once all day. And you weren't hovering outside my classroom to check up on me and ask if I parked under a streetlight and, damn it, I was worried."

He looked pleased, which annoyed her further.

"You were upset, huh?"

Exasperated, she put her hands on her hips. "G.T., why didn't you stop by after work? Why weren't you waiting in the hall by the classroom?"

He arched a brow. "I didn't know I was supposed to check in. Why were you worried, anyway? I'm a grown man. I can take care of myself."

She stared at him, taken aback. Is that what he thought? That this was all a one-way street? It was okay for him to be constantly checking up on her, but she wasn't to worry her little head over him? Well, to heck with that noise. She didn't need it and she didn't need him. Snapping the phone book shut with a decisive flick of her hand she said, "Now you know how it feels, don't you? Maybe now you'll be able to remember that while you're a grown man, I'm a grown woman. I can take care of myself, too." And she walked away.

G.T. was right behind her. "It's not the same thing, Claire. Not at all. Stop, will you? Hey, where are you going in such a hurry?"

She kept right on moving. "To buy myself an ice-cream bar. You ate mine, remember?"

"It was melting!"

"So I'll get myself a nice fresh cold one out of the ice-cream case."

"Claire, you're being very childish, running away from me like this."

"That's supposed to worry me? Isn't that the way you've seen me since day one? A child who needs constant checking on?"

"No," he exploded as they reached the cafeteria entrance. "Look," he finally said, running his hand through his hair. He pointed to a nearby empty table. "Just sit down over there, okay? I'll get your ice cream. You want the same bar as last time or something different?"

"I'm not sure. I think I want to look for myself."

He made an exaggerated sweeping gesture. "Well, far be it from me to cram my ice-cream choice down your throat. Is it permissible for me to escort you to the freezer while you make your choice? I can recommend the toasted almond. The one I ate was quite good."

"Oh, G.T., just sit down, will you? I look like a criminal with a cop on my tail."

"I don't tail crooks, Claire. Generally plainclothesmen do that. It's a little less obvious."

"Why are you still in your uniform, anyway? What have you been doing since three o'clock?" She'd baked chocolate-chip cookies and everything, she'd been so sure he'd stop by after all the hullabaloo of the evening before. "Did you keep your uniform on to impress some poor gullible female?"

He looked intrigued. "No, but it's not a half-bad idea. You know one I could try it out on?"

"Yeah, Wynetta."

Then he looked pained. "Oh, please."

She plunked a dollar bill down in front of the cashier before G.T. could get his wallet open. "I'm serious, G.T., where were you?"

He followed her back to the table, not much caring that he was going to be late getting back to class. "It was no big deal, honest. We were short a couple of guys today, that's all. I'm working a double shift. Officially I'm on an extended dinner break while I'm here for my class."

She was instantly horrified as she unwrapped her ice cream and took a bite. "You have to go back to work when you leave here tonight? A double shift? My gosh, you won't be done until, what, eleven o'clock?"

He pooh-poohed her concern. "Don't worry about it. I do it all the time— Oh, I get it. You're worried about being alone in the apartment tonight. I didn't have time to check. Has there been any sign of that creep today?" He watched her lick her lips, then swallow. He followed that bit of ice cream all the way down before dragging his eyes back to her face.

"Well the lady directly underneath me swears someone jiggled her back door knob around four this morning. She says she must have scared him off when she turned on all the lights because there was no one there when she finally got the courage to check." Claire made a dismissing gesture with her hand. "But she's always saying stuff like that. I think she's just being neurotic and it was probably the wind." No way would she admit to the frisson of fear that had snaked down her spine when her neighbor had imparted that bit of information.

G.T. looked unconvinced. "I'll come back again tonight," he decided on the spot. "Why don't you lie down on the living room sofa until I get there? That way you'll be able to hear me if I knock softly so as not to wake up the girls. Shouldn't be much later than eleven-thirty."

She licked the stick clean and G.T. was fascinated by that little pink tongue. He was disappointed when she wrapped the stick up in her napkin and set it down.

"I wasn't thinking about me," she protested. Although now that he'd brought up the subject, she realized it would take hours of questioning under a hot bright light before she'd admit how well she'd slept the night before.

But he wasn't listening. "It's not a problem. Just listen for me."

"I was thinking of you. That's a lot of time to put in. You've got to be tired and isn't that when it's possible to drop your guard? Misjudge a situation and end up hurt?" She glanced at her wrist and rose. She had to get back. Now if she could just convince G.T. to be reasonable—

He was firm. "When you hear the knock, use the chain until you're sure it's me. I'll stay another night or two."

"You'll get too tired."

"Not so pooped that I can't still protect you and the girls, don't worry."

"Would you listen to me for once? We're fine. I stopped at the library and got out a book on self-defense for women."

That stopped him. "A book? You think you're competent enough to defend yourself after spending a couple of hours reading a book?"

She refused to let him put her down and nodded definitively. "Yes. The author had a lot of good ideas for using everyday articles around the house to fend off an attacker. As a matter of fact, when I get undressed tonight I'm going to keep my bra on my nightstand instead of throwing it in the hamper. My book says they're generally made of very strong material and can be useful for strangling your assailant."

G.T.'s eyes bugged out at that. She was going to use her brassiere to bump off a would-be attacker? Good God, the only way it would work was if the creep was so astonished at the novelty of being mauled with an article of women's intimate wear that he died of the surprise. "What are you going to do if he breaks in before you get undressed? Say, 'Excuse me, sir, but in order to make this fair, I'll need something to defend myself with. Would you mind waiting just a moment while I whip off my bra?' I gotta tell you, Claire, very few of the lowlifes I've run into are inclined to be fair, and *none* of them are going to sit still long enough for you to wrap something like that around their neck."

Claire glanced around the hall they were walking down, embarrassed. Thank God they were almost to her classroom. "Would you please lower your voice? I promise you, I'll wrap my, uh, unmentionables around *your* neck if anybody overhears this." She opened the door to her class and slipped inside. "And *don't* stop over tonight or I'll use my *National Geo*s on you," she threatened as the door began to close.

"Your what?"

"Some cop you are. I bet you didn't know you can flick a magazine at somebody and give them a faceful of paper cuts, did you? And I just happen to have an entire stack of *National Geo*s on my sofa table."

The door slapped shut and G.T. was left staring at it, convinced one of them had gone mad. The woman was prepared to take on the world with her bra and a magazine. She needed help. *He* needed help if he was to make it through protecting her until she was back on an even keel. The entire situation was insane, and so was he. Because you know what? he asked himself as he stomped back down the hall, now thoroughly late for his own second half of class. The thought of being wrapped up in Claire's undies was not all that unappealing. Now *that* was worrisome.

Claire sat in her seat. Deciphering *Ives v. South Buffalo Railroad Co.* would be a piece of cake compared to figuring out her former brother-in-law. And she wished to God her professor would stop staring at her. Her hair had only been dyed a short while. Were her roots showing already? Self-consciously she ran her hand through her short, cropped hair and the man's eyes followed the movement.

Her eyes widened. No, it couldn't be. He wasn't *interested*, was he? Not in *her*. Maybe she had a bit of ice cream left around her mouth and G.T. hadn't seen fit to mention it. Probably thought it would be funny to let her go on that way.

Quickly she ran her tongue around her lips. The professor stuttered in the middle of a sentence and had to start over.

"Yes, as I was saying, in his closing arguments, Judge Werner—"

This was amazing. She would ask G.T. his opinion of the situation when he showed up tonight, as she had no doubt he would. He'd had a lot more experience with this kind of thing. He ought to be able to tell her if the man was interested or simply occasionally stuttered.

"He *what?*" G.T. roared later that evening.

"Shh, you'll wake the girls." Claire waved her hands at him in a frantic shushing motion.

"I'll do more than wake the girls if some bozo's coming on to you. I'll raise the damn rafters!" he threatened.

She snapped her fingers. "I forgot. I was going to check my hair in the mirror." Leaning toward G.T., she offered the top of her head to him. "Look here, G.T. Do I have roots showing already? Maybe that's why he was staring."

He gave her hair only a cursory glance, then turned his head away. She was too close. The perfume of her shampoo had invaded his nostrils, making him almost dizzy with the odor of ripe peach. Soft and sweet, like Claire, he thought, then closed his eyes in despair. Even his olfactory glands were betraying him. "Claire, if you didn't notice anything when you fixed your hair this morning, he sure as hell couldn't have seen anything from across the room this evening. Think about it."

"Well, it was just an idea."

A darn stupid one, although he left that unsaid. Claire had better hurry up and get her law degree. By the time he was done wiping up the floor with all the creeps he was bound to have to protect her from until she settled back down, he'd probably need a good attorney. It was sad, but some guys could smell a vulnerable woman from a mile away and they didn't hesitate to move right in and take advantage. This guy was a lawyer, to boot. Probably chased ambulances on the days he couldn't find any assailable females in his classroom.

Probably it would be best not to pursue this conversation right then, he realized. He was overtired from working the double shift and not in the best frame of mind. While another night on the cramped sofa held limited appeal, getting into an argument, when his mind was fogged with fatigue and he might inadvertently say something hurtful, was unthinkable. He never wanted to see her in pain again. "Listen, if you don't mind, I'm going to take a quick shower and grab a few hours of sleep. Maybe in the morning one of us will have some kind of brilliant mental revelation, but right now my brain's too fogged to function."

"Oh, I'm sorry. Sure. I didn't mean to keep you up or bother you with my questions. I mean, I was just wondering, that's all and—"

He kissed her forehead and was immediately sorry, because then his mouth was warmed up and it just wanted to keep on going. He touched two fingers to it in a warning gesture. It had better behave. "Tomorrow, okay?"

She backed away a step. "Right. Tomorrow. I'll just get you a towel and—"

"I know where everything is. Go on to bed."

"Oh. Well, all right, then. I'll just—"

"Go to bed. And quickly, before I give in to the temptation to come tuck you in."

"Yes. Uh, good night." She spun on her heel and fled into her bedroom.

G.T. smiled as the door clicked shut. She was aware of him. As a man, she was aware of him. He could tell. It was probably not a great idea, but still, it made him feel good to not be alone in his malady. He whistled softly as he entered the bathroom, but stopped a moment later. She'd left her unmentionables hanging from a hook on the back of the door.

Reverently he touched the lace and silk, running his hand over its softness. She may be temporarily running around in snug jeans, flashy silk poet blouses and snazzy little crocheted vest things, but here was the Claire he remembered. The pastel lace and ribbon woman.

His eyes widened as he fingered the delicate piece of female frippery. Claire's brassiere was covered with bright green splotches, he realized as his eyes really focused on the article in front of him. Wonderingly, he picked it off the hook and, dangling it by a strap, left the bathroom.

He knocked once on her bedroom door. "Claire?"

"Yes?" Her voice was soft, blurry with sleep already.

He wanted nothing more than to climb into the warm cocoon she'd created and slowly bring her back to awareness, an awareness of him. But this was killing him. He had to know. He opened the door and stepped inside her bedroom.

She sat up in bed, flicked on her bedside light, then blinked owlishly at him. "What's the matter? Did you hear somebody jiggling the door knob?"

"What? Good Lord, no. But just in case, I've brought you your ammunition. You left it in the bathroom." He crossed to the bed and gravely handed her the bit of underwear. "Claire, your bra has measles. Or chicken pox. Something."

She sighed and laughed ruefully. "You weren't supposed to see this. Nobody was."

"Why?" he asked suspiciously. "It's not catching, is it?"

She really did laugh then. "No, it's just embarrassing, is all. I got thrown out of the Laundromat over this."

"Claire, I know it's late and you're tired, but try and be coherent for just a few seconds here. Who threw you out of the Laundromat and why didn't you call me? I'd have taken care of them for you."

She shook her head. "No, it was all my fault. *Somebody,* and let me assure you they will each go to their graves protesting their own innocence, *somebody* had a green crayon in one of her pockets. It melted in the dryer all over a load of whites and the inside of the dryer. The manager of the Laundromat was not pleased, let me tell you."

He imagined not, but that was his Claire, he realized. This bit of feminine frippery was a good representation of the many contradictory facets of her personality. A lacy symbol of her quintessential femininity, it nonetheless had the character to withstand the assault of motherhood, represented by the green crayon, and the hidden strength to keep guard on her nightstand every evening, taking a stand in the defense of her little family. It was actually a very noble piece of underwear. Some anthropological study ought to be done, in fact, studying the survival time of cultures where the women wore brassieres versus those where they hung free, so to speak. Freud would have loved Claire's bra, he decided.

"Was he able to clean the crayon out of the dryer?" he asked with a sort of morbid fascination.

"Eventually, yes. But I don't go there anymore."

"I can see where it might be awkward." He cleared his throat. "Anyway, here it is." He set it on the nightstand and turned to leave. Claire looked too darn provocative propped up against her pillow, rumpled sheets twined around her. He needed to get out of there.

"G.T.?"

"Yes?"

"Can I ask you something?"

Reluctantly he turned back. "Sure." But only if you hurry.

"If you were a man—"

If he was a man?

"And you wanted to attack me—"

Had she read his mind?

"Would you rather have me defend myself by trying to strangle you with this?" She pointed to the nightstand. "Or the book also suggests shoving your keys up an assailant's nose. What do you think?"

His eyes opened wide. What? "Well, to tell you the truth, I've never given the matter much—"

"On the one hand, while the keys sound a lot more painful—they're only disabling, if you know what I mean—whereas throttling the poor guy might not hurt as much, but it would be a lot more permanent, which isn't really what I want, is it? All I actually need is enough time to get away, like you said."

"Claire—"

"Then again, if I don't keep the keys right in my purse where I always know where they are, I'll always be looking for them. Probably lock myself out, too, if I go out and forget to check for them. And how much consideration does an attacker deserve, anyway? Maybe I should just go ahead and choke him." She looked up at him expectantly.

He glanced from her curious face to the green-spotted bra next to her and back. He was speechless, so he pivoted on his heel and made his escape. "I'll think about it while I shower," he offered, feeling somewhat dazed by the conversation. "Give you my decision in the morning."

He closed her door with exaggerated care and went into the bathroom. Maybe the steam would clear his brain.

Chapter Eight

G.T. stopped by the next afternoon after his shift ended. Claire met him at the door, tapped her foot and assured him of their continued well being—which he figured she knew he could see for himself—so it was obvious she understood the reason for the casual drop by and was annoyed. He hung around for as long as he dared, but he knew she'd never put up with him staying over again.

Arnie called as he was thinking about leaving—Claire and the little girls were yawning in his face. At the sound of G.T.'s voice, Arnie demanded to know what he was doing there. G.T. informed him of the situation while secretly worrying over how possessive Arnie still sounded.

Always before, he'd thought it was cute to watch Arnie dealing with his two small daughters, but that night it annoyed him no end to have to hand over the phone and let Melissa and Chrissie chat. He worried about how possessive *he* was beginning to feel.

He listened while Missy told her father about that day's show-and-tell. They'd been supposed to bring something to do with water. The teacher had suggested a toy boat or maybe a rubber ducky, but most the kids had decided to show off water tricks. Geraldine McCandlish's experiment hadn't worked right. Her pants had gotten all wet in the ensuing mess and she'd had to spend the rest of the afternoon in her tights and shirt until her mother had shown up with a dry pair. And you could see her *underwear* through her tights. Then she told him about her own experiment.

G.T. wanted to grab the phone and tell him he was getting old news. G.T. had heard that story hours ago. In fact, it had been G.T. who'd thought of the simple experiment Missy had performed. Furthermore, in case Arnie hadn't realized it, his daughter was a damn quick study. She'd pulled off the demonstration without a hitch. Somehow he managed to control himself.

Then Chrissie got on the phone. She described the chocolate cake she'd helped her mother bake that afternoon.

Would it be totally immature to rip the phone out of the three-year-old's hand and inform his older brother he'd already eaten two pieces and it was highly doubtful there'd be any left by the time Arnie arrived the following weekend? He sighed. Very likely. Instead, he went out to the kitchen where he couldn't hear any more of the conversation and cut himself a third slice. It actually was quite good. He pulled a gallon of milk out of the refrigerator. There was something about chocolate and milk that just went together. No matter how old you got, you never outgrew it, either. Sort of like a good marriage, he theorized as he licked a finger and used it to pick up crumbs off the counter. He popped the crumb-laden finger back into his mouth, then sopped up some more.

Yes, a good marriage was like chocolate and milk. Very different from each other, but totally complementary. And you never got sick of it. Not now, not twenty years from now. Claire was like chocolate cake. Sweet, but not cloying. Arnie, on the other hand, was no glass of milk. Instead of balancing their marriage with some wholesome solidity, he'd been a cup of coffee or a tumbler of cola. A quick jolt of caffeine, a little effervescence, then... low blood sugar.

After that night and over the next month, he'd stopped by a couple of times a week and shared his class break time with Claire when they overlapped out at Oakley, but he remained more or less circumspect, uneasy with the tangle of emotions he experienced more and more frequently around Claire.

Then came the night in late October when Claire verbally tackled him in the Oakley hallway.

"G.T., I'm so glad you didn't cut class tonight. I really need you."

She did? A rush of adrenaline flooded his system. Hot damn.

"A guy in my class asked me to go hear a blues band with him tomorrow night. They're playing at some bar down in new town. I told him sure only I just now remembered my baby-sitter has another permanent sitting job on Fridays. G.T., this means a lot to me. Please, please, please could you stay with the girls tomorrow night while I go out? I'd feel a lot better if the girls were with somebody they knew. Please? It's my first real date in gosh, six or seven years."

It was all he could do to keep his jaw up. She needed him—to baby-sit? While she went out with some *other* guy? Some guy he'd never met? Some guy neither he nor in all likelihood Claire knew anything about? Some guy who planned to take her to a bar? Who planned to seduce her? And he was sure that was all the man had in mind. G.T. was a male himself, after all. He knew these things.

"G.T.?"

He stared blankly at her for a moment. "I'm thinking," he explained, finally. "My calendar's at home. I'll have to check it and—"

"You don't know if you have a date for tomorrow night?" She'd spent the last several weeks trying to reign in her subconscious and all the romantic fantasies involving G.T. It was constantly allowing to perk up into her mind at inappropriate times. Meanwhile he had so many dates he couldn't keep track of them? A lesser woman might be upset, even angry that she'd allowed herself to fantasize over such a man. Claire, however, with her newfound ability to take control of her life would blot out whatever unworthy pangs of hurt she felt with her date tomorrow night.

Of course he knew he had no date for the following evening, unless you counted the one with the Laundromat. He hadn't tangoed with a washing machine in two weeks. He was either going to have to stop at the mall and buy some more socks or squeeze in some time with a washer and dryer real soon. It was a sad, sad commentary on his current mental condition that he hadn't been able to work up much enthusiasm for a rendezvous with the opposite sex for over a month now. Oh, he'd had invitations, which was what made it all the worse. This was by his own choice that his hot date with a couple of overgrown appliances was about as exciting as his social life got lately.

What was wrong with him? Claire obviously wasn't having a problem getting her life back together. Look at her, all eager and excited over going out on the town tomorrow night. But wasn't that what he'd wanted?

Of course!

Aargh. He clamped his teeth shut. It was the only way he refrained from asking her exactly how much she knew about this man who'd asked her out. She'd accuse him of being overprotective again, of trying to insulate her from "the real world."

Sounded like a damn fine idea to him. He'd never understood the motive behind the Rapunzel story before. But now, well, given access to a pile of stones, he'd have Claire installed up in a tower in no time flat.

A new worry hit like a ton of bricks. He'd never gotten around to teaching Claire the self-defense tricks he'd promised, and it wasn't strictly because he didn't want Arnie accusing him of *overreacting*. He grimaced as he thought of how Mr. Big Brawny Cop was afraid of what would happen if he started touching that creamy smooth skin of hers again while he demonstrated how to break an assailant's hold.

Well, if he couldn't touch Claire's soft skin, no way was Harvey Lawyer Wanna-be going to be allowed to touch it either. It was G.T.'s fault Claire still didn't know how to protect herself, although he knew better than to say so. His eyes narrowed thoughtfully. It would be awful tough for Mr. Suave to put the moves on Claire if he found G.T. ensconced on the sofa when he brought her home tomorrow night. He could protect Claire without saying a word. She'd never even know.

"Tell you what," he offered magnanimously. "I'll cancel whatever's on my calendar. I can tell this is important to you and I'll feel better myself if I'm the one staying with the girls after that trouble your friend Wynetta had last month."

Claire beamed and reached up impulsively to kiss him on the cheek. She felt that same disturbing buzz, but it no longer concerned her so much. She'd thought this all carefully through and decided that G.T. had this strange effect on her and figured so predominantly in her dreams because he was the only male she'd had much contact with in a very long time. She'd take care of that problem starting tomorrow night.

It was a shame she'd had to ask him to baby-sit as it might be a bit awkward introducing her former brother-in-law to her date. Still, though, this was best. G.T. was the only one she'd really trust to stay with the girls until after midnight. Claire didn't stop to question why that was. She knew. G.T. would go to the wall for them. He'd protect any member of her little family with his life.

She suspected he might be going a bit overboard, however, when G.T. showed up at six o'clock the following night in full uniform, gun and handcuffs included. She followed him from the front door to the living room where she cocked her head while she studied him once he'd sprawled out on her sofa. "Didn't you get off at three today?" she asked.

G.T. smiled benignly and spread his arms across the sofa back. "Yes, I did as a matter of fact. Why?"

"That was three hours ago," Claire pointed out. "Couldn't you have chucked at least your gun in all that time?"

"I had to stop by the mall and buy some socks."

"That accounts for at least fifteen minutes of the three hours."

He shrugged innocently. "There were a few other errands I needed to take care of as well."

Claire tapped her foot in unworthy suspicion. "Uh-huh."

"I wanted to get in here in plenty of time," he told her innocently. "So you wouldn't worry."

If that was the truth, he'd missed his mark. She was plenty worried over this whole evening. Did she really want to do this? She'd known all along she'd eventually have to get back into the whole dating thing. And it had to be now. This problem of fixating on G.T. needed to be solved. The only way to do that, she'd decided, was to expose herself to a few other examples of the male half of the species. See if she couldn't convince her subconscious to fixate on one of them for a while.

So why did he have to show up in his uniform, she wailed silently. He looked so good in blue. She shouldn't feel this thrill at the mere sight of him, she really shouldn't, because no matter what he said, Claire knew G.T. meant to intimidate her date. Why hadn't she thought of that possibility last night? Mostly because she'd figured G.T. would be grateful to see her going out again. After all, the more independent she became the quicker he could get on with his life. She hated that he saw her as a responsibility, and Claire was sure he did. "You'd better behave," she warned.

"Who me? I always behave."

Not from what she'd heard. Still, he had cancelled his date for her and she was behaving ungraciously. "You need some dinner?" she asked.

"No, I'm fine," he assured her with a polite smile. "I managed to grab a hamburger as I did my running around. Didn't want to put you to any extra work while you were getting ready for your big date."

Oh, sure. Make her feel small.

G.T. turned on the lamp next to the sofa. "Kind of dark in here, isn't it? Wouldn't want your date to think you can't pay your electrical bill."

The low-lighted, soft mood she'd taken pains to create was immediately destroyed. Every crack in the plaster walls and ceiling was thrown into glaring relief along with the flaws in her plans for the evening.

This was never going to work. Not in a million years. How could she concentrate on anything other than G.T. when he was sitting right there looking incredibly virile and masculine? She couldn't even remember clearly what her date looked like. He'd been just sort of—average. What was she going to do? Introduce the girls and G.T. to the first nondescript male to ring the doorbell? Oh, Lord, had she even told Rob about the girls? She couldn't remember.

You know, she'd read articles in the women's magazines written by divorcees. They'd shared their frustrations and concerns over the difficulties they'd had getting their feet wet again in the dating world after fifteen to twenty years of marriage and not worrying about who paid for what and what was expected of whom at the end of the night.

She'd only been out of circulation five years. Wasn't even back in circulation yet, not really, and she was already falling apart. She felt a whole new wave of sympathy for those faceless women.

"Where are the girls?" G.T. finally asked. He was doing his best to protect Claire while being supportive of her attempts to get on with her life after the ego bashing she'd taken from Arnie, but this was killing him. "I'll give them their bath and read to them so you can concentrate on your make-up and stuff." He pointed at the neckline of her low-cut poet's blouse. "You are going to change, aren't you? It looks like you've got a button missing."

Claire looked down to study her neckline. She fingered each button as she checked it. "Chrissie and Missy are in their room. They've already had their bath and are putting on their jammies." She finished her inspection and looked up. "My buttons are fine. There's nothing wrong with my blouse."

G.T. nodded agreeably. "Oh." She wasn't going out of here in that low-cut thing she had on. Not unless her date wanted to leave a cash deposit behind with G.T. . . . A nonrefundable one if the goods came back late or damaged. "Still, you might want to change anyway because it *looks* like there should be at least two or three more because of the funny way it hangs."

"That's ridiculous." But she looked doubtfully back down. G.T. was probably just giving her a hard time. But on the off chance that he wasn't, she switched shirts.

After over an hour of fiddling with her clothes and her face, Rob rang the bell. She opened the door and was pleased to recognize him. *Yes*, she told herself. *That's what he looks like. This is him.* She all but pulled him into the room, such was her relief. Claire introduced Rob to G.T. Other than shaking her date's hand, Claire noticed, G.T.'s own hand rested over his gun the entire time.

G.T. made a production out of writing down the name of the bar they were going to—for emergencies, he was sure Rob would understand. And asked what time he could expect them back. Claire got the impression if they were more than ten minutes late, he'd come looking for them. She got Rob out of there as quickly as possible.

G.T. stared at the door Claire and her date had shut in his face for several moments, his hands clenched into fists. He'd done what he could to protect her. He'd attempted to—subtly so as not to tick off Claire, but not so subtly old buddy Rob missed the point— instill the fear of the Lord into him. There was nothing left to do but wait. The fear for her safety was valid, he acknowledged as he flexed his fists once more.

Rational fears he could handle. What was driving him crazy was the totally irrational stab of out-and-out green jealousy he was trying to beat into submission there in front of the door.

"Uncle G.T.?"

"Yeah, honey bunch?"

"Will you read Chrissie and me a story?"

G.T. dragged his eyes away from the door and down to the munchkin pulling on his pants leg. "Sure. What'd you have in mind?"

"*Toaster and Maureen go to Kindergarten*. Their fairy godmother fixes it so that they get to send their teacher, Miss Beasley, to the corner for some time-out. When Maureen comes home, her mother takes the teacher's side, so the fairy godmother sends her mother for time-out too. Mommy helped me write it this afternoon."

"Have a rough day at school this morning, did you, sweet cheeks?"

"Krysta Bianco told Miss Beasley I pushed her and I had to go to time-out."

"Did you push?"

"She pushed me first."

"Uh-huh. And when you came home, your mom told you no pushing no matter what?" G.T. hazarded a guess. "How'd you get Mommy to write down a story where she gets sent to time-out?"

Melissa pushed the large type computer printout at him. "She had to. At kindergarten open house last month, Miss Beasley told all the parents us kids would learn to read much faster if somebody spent some time every day taking our dic—dic—"

"Dictation?" G.T. flipped through the pages he'd taken. Yes, there was a crayon embellishment of the manuscript featuring his Claire sitting in a corner. It was hard to tell from the primitive drawing, but he believed she was sucking her thumb.

"Yeah, that. It means she's got to write down everything I say just the way I say it so I can learn to be a good reader."

"I see," G.T. said. And he did see a lot of things. He saw that Claire had her hands full with this one, that was for sure. He also saw that she was a good parent who wasn't afraid of disciplining but also knowledgeable and mature enough to know a child had to work off the anger somehow. She hadn't minded being the butt of Maureen's and Toaster's pranks. Claire had no doubt recognized that a story was a fairly innocuous way for her daughter to work things out.

If Claire could be a good sport, so could he. G.T. read to them, gave them a snack, oversaw teethbrushing and prayers. He tucked them and several stuffed animals in and checked the closet and under the bed for monsters before turning off the light. He left the door open several inches so he could hear them. Then he planted himself in front of the television while he waited.

At twenty after twelve he got up long enough to start the coffeemaker.

At twelve-thirty he heard a key turn in the lock.

"We're back," Claire called as she pushed the front door open. "Everything go okay?"

"Of course," G.T. said as he rose from the sofa. "You know I never have any trouble with Chrissie and Melissa."

"You always say that," Claire said as she fell into G.T.'s game of casting Rob as the outsider without even realizing it. "You've either got a golden touch that I wish to God I had, or you lie like a rug."

G.T. shrugged and didn't comment. "Well, don't leave your friend out in the hall," he admonished. "Bring him in. I started some coffee a few minutes ago. It should be just about ready."

Claire studied her former brother-in-law until something clicked. "You changed your clothes," she said as G.T. played the gracious host—and it didn't escape her notice that he was playing gracious host in *her* apartment as she and Rob were ushered into her own living room. "Did you have them in your car?"

He looked down at his soft flannel shirt and casual jeans. "What? Oh, no. Don't you remember? I must have left them here last time I stayed overnight. I found them in the linen closet."

Claire's smile became a bit grim. She wished the jeans and shirt had stayed lost in the back of the closet. She wished G.T. would get lost, followed immediately out the door by Bob. Rob. Whatever. G.T. was making it sound as though he was a frequent overnight guest. She would kill him when they were finally alone.

She'd tried so hard to blot out thoughts of G.T. while struggling to hear Rob over the unbelievably loud music they'd listened to that she'd given herself a headache. The way she felt right now, it should only be terminal. There was nothing wrong with Rob—he was a little bland, but a good doctor and a personality transplant would take care of that. But then, G.T. could use one of those too, and while he could madden her in nothing flat, she always enjoyed being with him. Rob hadn't angered her, not at all. In fact, he seemed kind of blah when she compared him to G.T.

Oh, damn and blast. Her date had done nothing to exorcise G.T. from her brain. In fact, Rob had made G.T. look even better. Darn the man!

Still, she was mad at him and two weeks went by before she caved into pressure from Chrissie and Melissa.

"G.T., the girls want you to come for dinner tomorrow night," Claire told him one night as they sat together during their break. "They want to have a barbecue."

"They want to grill out? In October?"

She shrugged. "I told them it was too cold, but they really have their hearts set on it."

He sighed. Claire had really asked very little of him lately. The few things he insisted on, like seeing her to her car after class, she resisted like crazy. A less secure man might feel insulted. Fortunately G.T. was above all that. Certainly he got a little irritated with her recalcitrance from time to time, but that was only to be expected. Heck, she could be a little more gracious with her refusals, couldn't she? He'd done nothing more than buss her on the cheek since that night last month. He was safe, do you hear? Safe. And believe him, it was killing G.T. not to know if Rob or some other guy he didn't even know about might be getting away with more than that. How much more? Damn, he was driving himself crazy. "Okay, but they'll really have to bundle up. You don't want them getting sick, you know."

Claire rolled her eyes.

"I saw that."

"I'd have to roll them continuously for ten years to get even halfway caught up with your side of the family."

"Oh, hah. Just tell me where we're going to freeze our butts off and catch pneumonia. And let me forewarn you, I'm not going to any forest preserve that only has outhouses. It has to at least have a heated john."

"I have no intention of jeopardizing anyone's health," she informed him superiorly as she polished off the last of her toasted-almond ice-cream bar. "Except possibly yours, of course."

He glowered. "How come mine gets jeopardized and you three get off scot-free?"

"Because I was talking about the little grill I keep in my storage space in the apartment building basement. We'll just put it out behind the building. I'll keep the girls safe and warm inside while you do your thing out there. You done with your coffee? I've got to get back."

"Wait a minute. How come I get stuck out there while you're inside? I'm the invited guest," he reminded her, feeling compelled to argue with her apparent sexist stance. She was being appallingly unliberated about all this. And *where* had she gotten that bodysuit she was wearing with her jeans tonight? Deceptively simple and demure with its long sleeves and scoop neck, it molded itself to her torso so intimately she had the appearance of an incredibly sexy cat burglar. The judges of the world were literally going to have to put on the blindfold of justice when Claire hit their courtroom. Otherwise they'd all turn into babbling idiots.

Claire spread her hands wide as she rose to her feet, unaware—thankfully, from G.T.'s perspective—of what she was doing to him. "Hey, it's not that I'd mind doing it myself. I'd be *happy* to do the grilling. I managed to pull it off quite successfully several times last summer."

The expression on her face was difficult for G.T. to read. Maybe it was sincere, then again...

"It's just that I happen to know from real-life experience that if a man is within a two-hundred-foot radius of a lighted grill, some kind of as-yet-undiscovered male hormone gets triggered and they feel absolutely compelled to take over." She picked up her texts off the cafeteria table as G.T. stared up into her face. "So why should I do all the dirty work—struggling to get the charcoal lighted, taking a chance on blowing myself up with the lighter fluid, which would leave my two poor babies motherless—only to have you take all the glory?"

You know, the workings of the feminine mind was a fascinating thing, G.T. decided as he watched Claire walk away before he'd thought of a proper rebuttal. That damn plaid bodysuit had left him temporarily witless, he guessed. And while there was no way to prove it, he was fairly certain he'd just been royally had. A male hormone that switched on at the smell of charcoal? He didn't think so.

He finished off his coffee and stood before taking the empty cup to the trash can. The whole thing sounded more to him like a racket thought up by a bunch of extremely clever and manipulative females who all wore too-snug bodysuits and were intent on taking it easy while appearing to kowtow to the male ego.

Chapter Nine

To let her get away with it or not, that was the question. There'd yet to be a decision reached when he maneuvered his car into a spot half a block down from Claire's apartment the next evening. He walked to her entrance and his eyes narrowed.

"What's he doing here?" he growled to himself as he frowned at his brother's car. "What is this, some kind of family get-together she's got planned for tonight? Well, I'm not cooking Arnie's supper, that's for damn sure. He can freeze his butt off grilling his own damn burger."

He gestured to Arnie's subtly toned gold sports car. "Look at that, would you? Guy buys a beautiful expensive car like that and doesn't even bother to make sure it's parked legally. His front end is at least three, four feet into the crosswalk. Why, I could call in and have him towed."

He thought about that. That would really be evil, wouldn't it?

Evil, but funny. At least, from his point of view.

Arnie would be superpissed.

His mother would probably never speak to him again.

Neither one of those constituted any great tragedy, he decided. He'd convinced his mother to visit one lost relative after another once she'd come back from her month in Hawaii. He'd barely seen her since late August.

G.T. stood there on the sidewalk, contemplating his brother's car.

The tow hook might scratch the paint. Naw, it wasn't worth it. However, now that he thought about it, he did have his ticket book in his glove compartment. Since he was responsible for every ticket in there, he never let it get too far out of his sight.

Now *that* was a real possibility. Arnie would be mad, but him being such a hotshot lawyer, all it would take would be a couple of phone calls to wiggle his way out of it. He probably wouldn't even have to pay the fine. G.T. would only be causing his brother a minor inconvenience and it would sure make G.T.'s evening.

Heck, if he slurred his handwriting when he wrote his badge number, Arnie wouldn't even know he was the officer responsible for the dastardly deed, not that Arnie would recognize his badge number if it snuck up from behind and bit him on the butt, anyway.

It was really too good an opportunity to pass up.

"This kind of chance doesn't come along every day of the week," he told himself as he walked back to his car and retrieved his ticket book.

He wrote out the citation there, out of view of Claire's windows. It wouldn't do for Claire to glance out the window and see him. She wouldn't understand. Once he got rid of Arnie tonight, he would take great pleasure in spelling out exactly how a man got turned on. For crying out loud, she was convinced male hormones turned on at the sight of a lump of charcoal. And he would advise her that if she didn't care for what she learned, there was little she could do about it. Should she go so far as to shave her head and start wearing studded leather, there was something so essentially feminine about her, he doubted he'd be able to ignore her lure. Certainly her brassy blond short hair and garish earrings had done little to temper his libido. He didn't *like* them, but he had no problem seeing through them, either.

He slipped the book back into his glove compartment and surreptitiously glanced up to check Claire's windows as he approached his brother's car and slipped the ticket under his wiper blade.

Damn, that felt good.

He chuckled all the way into the entry foyer.

"Yes?"

"It's me, Claire, G.T."

"Oh. Hi. Hang on a second and I'll buzz you in."

G.T. frowned. She sounded distracted. Like she was surprised or something that he was there. What the heck, she was the one who'd invited him over. Had she forgotten already? Women. Who could read them?

Several seconds went by before Claire got around to releasing the lock on the inner door, and G.T. took the stairs two at a time up to her level. He'd feel better once he got a good look at her face, know what was going on then. Claire was lousy at hiding her emotions. It was one of the reasons, one of the *many* reasons, he didn't think she'd make a very good lawyer—unless, of course, she wore that new bodysuit of hers to court. Then she'd get away with anything she wanted to.

He turned the corner at her landing. Arnie better not be trying to intimidate her. The front door had been left ajar for him. He strode into the apartment, into the living room.

"Hi, Uncle G.T., how're you doin'?"

G.T. ran his hand through the hair of the midget who'd just tackled his knee. "Hi, pumpkin puss, I'm doing fine. How're you?"

"Good. I'm so glad you camed! Mommy 'n' Missy 'n' me made brownies 'cause we knowed they was your favorites."

"Know what?" he asked as he took in Arnie sitting on Claire's living room sofa, an ankle propped on a knee, his thin black socks snug, not showing the slightest wrinkle at his ankle—how did he do that? But where was Claire?

"What?" Chrissie's angelic little face glowed up at him.

"You were right. Brownies are my favorite."

"I know," the child admitted smugly. "You told us about a hunnert times."

"That many?" Damn it, where was she?

"At least."

"Guess you got the message, huh?" He pried her loose before he lost the circulation in his leg and lifted her into his arms. Big mistake. The child wrapped her arms around his neck and hugged him hard enough to affect the blood flow to his brain. He put up with it, though. Let Arnie see how unnecessary he really was.

"Uncle G.T., you're here!" Missy cried as she hurtled into the room and attached herself lampreylike to the leg he'd just freed.

"Hi, snookums. Got a kiss for your favorite uncle?" After he leaned down to receive the wet smack and let Missy's pigtails brush the floor long enough for a happy shriek or two, he greeted his brother. "Arnie."

Arnie drummed his fingers on his raised knee and gave him a sardonic smirk as he nodded his head in acknowledgment of the greeting. "G.T. Been making yourself at home, I see."

He shrugged. "They needed somebody."

"And my ever noble brother naturally jumped right in to fill the perceived gap, hmm? Don't you ever get tired of playing Dudley Do-right?"

G.T. decided to ignore him. He'd have the last laugh when Arnie went downstairs and found the parking ticket, so he directed his attention back to the girls. "Where's your mom, ladies? I need to talk to her about this infamous barbecue she's got planned." And to reassure himself that she was all right. She really had sounded funny on the intercom.

He found her out in the kitchen grinding dried onion-soup mix into a bowl of ground meat with her bare hands. Good thing the hamburger was already dead, otherwise it would be screaming in agony about now. "Maybe it just can't find the white flag," he suggested as he came up behind her, "but I'm sure it gives up."

She jumped. "What? Oh, G.T., it's you."

"How many other people have you buzzed in in the past few minutes?"

"Hmm? Oh, none. Arnie came a while ago. Why do you ask?"

He sighed. "Never mind." He watched as she continued to beat the hamburger meat into submission. "You seem preoccupied, honey. Something bothering you?"

"No, everything's fine."

One thing the police force had taught him was patience. He didn't have long to wait. Her words whistled out like steam from a kettle.

"I just don't understand why he's here."

Him being Arnie, he assumed.

"I mean it's hardly *my* fault he broke up with his little paralegal. My understanding was they had things in common they could use as the basis to build a relationship, unlike us. He could *talk* to her. Makes you wonder what he ever saw in me, doesn't it?"

He'd seen her sweetness and naïveté. Qualities as rare as his chance of making police chief. Now was not the time to point that out to Claire, however. G.T. doubted she'd see either of those two attributes as anything but the handicap she was doing her damnedest to disguise with her red minis and brassy dye job. Arnie had seen them, recognized their worth and grabbed them. Only then he hadn't known what to do with them and he'd thrown them away. G.T. wasn't so stupid. He just hoped that, with Claire in law school now and better able to *communicate* with her former spouse, Arnie wasn't getting any ideas.

"It was all right when he came and took the girls every other weekend. I was coping. But now... Is he going to just show up like this several nights a week and stay here? He's making small talk, cracking jokes about when he was in law school like all of the sudden we have something in common. The girls weren't enough? What is happening here? Is he waiting for me to put dinner on the table like when we were married? Darn it, I don't want him here, and if he brought a bag of dirty laundry with him I'll just spit. There were times before I realized he'd found Suzy Paralegal that I wondered, if I dropped off the face of the earth would he miss me before he ran out of clean underwear? Or maybe he'd run out of socks first and notice then, I don't know—"

G.T. reached out and put his hands on her shoulders to steady her. He drew her backward into his chest. "Claire, Claire, calm down, honey. You're getting all worked up, maybe over nothing. He hasn't got the sense to appreciate a gem like you. Maybe his little paralegal will come back and they'll make up. Or he'll get assigned another assistant. Or check this out, his cases will be assigned to some female judge. There are all kinds of possibilities out there."

She sniffed and looked helplessly at her fat-coated palms. Finally she blotted her eyes with the backs of her hands. "What you're saying is that if he did come back, I haven't got what it takes to hang on to him."

G.T. rolled his eyes. It was all right. He was behind her and she couldn't see. He hadn't handled that one very well. Well, he'd never pretended to be a shrink. He went on the defensive. "So you want him back?"

Horrified at the prospect, she immediately denied it. "No!"

"Well, then?"

"It's the principle of the thing." This time she rubbed the end of her nose with the back of her fist. She leaned into him and he rubbed her upper arms for her. "Sometimes I think about how nice it would be if he tried to come back, but that was just so I could tell him to drop dead."

That was a relief. "Oh, I see. Not too vindictive, are we? Will it help if I tell you I wrote him a parking ticket on my way up here?"

She laughed involuntarily. "You didn't."

He crossed his fingers over her heart. His was covered. "God's truth."

"You're bad."

"Yeah." If only she knew how bad he wanted to get, too. "Now what do you say we get these burgers moving?"

Halfheartedly, she removed a wad of meat from the bowl and began to shape it. "He says he wants to spend more time with his children, but it could be more than that, don't you think? I mean, do you think it would be bad if we ended up getting back together for the kids' sake?"

G.T. was appalled. It would be horrible. Had she no self-respect at all? He had liked it a lot better when she was wanting to tell Arnie to drop dead. Writing his jerk of a brother a ticket had been no more than a mosquito bite compared to what he deserved. But the size proboscis a mosquito would need to puncture Arnie's giant ego would be of heavy-duty proportion in the extreme. But, G.T. thought, if he ever came up with a way to bring his big brother down to size, man, let this be fair warning, stay out of his way because he'd be off and running in less time than it took a well-connected hooker to post bail. "We can talk about this later," he informed her grimly, needing time to sort out his own messy thoughts. "Meanwhile, you go light the grill. You're doing the barbecuing tonight."

"Me?"

"Yeah, you. I'll set the table and have Arnie make the salad."

Her brows really rose at that. "Arnie's going to make the salad?"

"If he wants to eat any of it."

"Huh. This I've got to see. Did I tell you he doesn't like my red skirt?"

Arnie probably didn't want anybody else seeing Claire's gorgeous legs. G.T. knew how he felt. Claire was the kind of woman a man wanted to hide in an Arabian purdah lest some other male see what he had and steal her away. G.T., however, wasn't so stupid as to admit he and Arnie had anything in common. Instead he said, "His taste has always been all in his mouth."

Claire shaped a third burger and added it to the small pile on the plate. "What if I burn them?"

"You won't. We're going to show Arnie the new, competent and in-control you, all right?"

She seemed dazed by the suggestion. "Yeah, I guess."

Arnie was informed of the new house rules and reluctantly rose from the sofa to come help. It didn't take long for dinner to get organized with three cooks working on it. Long before G.T. was ready, they were seated at the table passing condiments and making chilled but polite conversation. It amazed him to watch Claire interact with her former spouse. The vibrant woman who slept with her attack brassiere at her side, the lady who'd argue loud and long over him buying her a lousy ice-cream bar, was nowhere to be found. Instead, there was a mouse, a little, timid gray mouse looking as if she were dressed for Halloween with her garish short hair and clothes. Heck, even her voice had gone all tentative tonight. Let's face it, the woman's wattage was down low and, as far as G.T. was concerned, Arnie was to blame.

"Good salad," Claire mumbled as she chewed a mouthful of lettuce.

"Thanks." Her former husband grunted. He bit into his burger.

It sounded sardonic to her, but with Arnie it was hard to tell. Maybe he really was grateful. Without knowing, it was difficult to respond and the small conversational gambit died.

She was sorry she'd invited G.T. No, she wasn't. She was only sorry Arnie had stopped by and ruined the evening she and the girls had so carefully planned. Feeling miserable, she bit into her hamburger. Instant relief. It was good. Nothing for Arnie to criticize. Hah, take that, turkey. I don't need you to flip my burgers, I can flip 'em myself.

Ordinarily she'd take a great deal of satisfaction in having done it herself. Tonight all she felt was disappointment. She knew she'd been slightly off the wall since the divorce, but G.T. had never wavered. He'd been there for her whether she'd wanted him there or not, teasing the little girls, and, well, just being a rock.

A couple of weeks ago, she would have insisted on doing the grilling herself. To prove a point. She'd really wanted to manipulate things so that G.T. could have taken over tonight without feeling as if he was stepping on her toes. It was to have been her payback of sorts for all the support he'd given. Barbecuing really was a guy thing. It must have killed him to stand aside and let her do it. But as long as he had she wasn't above rubbing it in a little bit.

"The meat turned out all right, don't you think?" she asked, intending to force a compliment. She knew it was more than all right. Arnie was already spreading mustard on his second bun.

"I suppose," Arnie admitted reluctantly. "Be a lot better if you could have gotten some fresh tomatoes to slice."

"It's the middle of October," G.T. jumped in and pointed out. "The only ones that're available are those gross hothouse things that come in a plastic tube. You know you hate hothouse tomatoes, so quit being difficult."

"I am not being difficult. I merely pointed out—"

"It won't kill you to give a well-deserved compliment, Arnie. Try repeating after me, 'Claire, this hamburger is delicious. I haven't had anything barbecued since the end of August and this really hits the spot.'" G.T. arched his brow at his brother, daring him to repeat it.

"You have really flipped out, you know that? I said the hamburger was okay, didn't I? Now get off my case or I'll tell Mom you look stressed. She'll come home from wherever it is she is now and spend the weekend to take care of you." His eyes swept the length of the table and lit on his youngest daughter. "Put your napkin in your lap, Chrissie. That's where it goes during a meal."

Chrissie looked to her mother for confirmation and Claire nodded. "Daddy's right, honey. Your napkin belongs in your lap. Need some help shaking it out?"

Her words tore at G.T.'s heart. He was the outsider here when you came right down to it. Arnie was their father and always would be no matter how much G.T. wished it otherwise.

"Stop babying her, Claire," Arnie directed. "She's a big girl. She can shake out her napkin for herself."

But Claire had had enough. Her evening had been ruined and she was in no mood to kowtow to the man who'd wrecked it. "Arnie, if you expect me not to contradict your instructions to the children, you'll have to refrain from correcting me in front of them."

"Don't be silly. There's a difference here. You could hardly not back me up. I was right. You, on the other hand—"

She was firm. "If you ever correct me or downgrade me in front of them again, I will do the same. Life is a two-way street and you better stay on your own side and not cross the double yellow. You do and you might get your toes run over. In fact, I can pretty well guarantee it."

Arnie's jaw dropped, but he said nothing when Claire shook out Chrissie's napkin and patted it into her lap.

G.T., on the other hand, wanted to jump up and shout something along the lines of, *Hurray and hallelujah!* Look at her. Her oversize goofy earrings absolutely quivered with her indignation. Wasn't she spectacular? Maybe he'd been wrong all along. She just might make a heck of a lawyer, after all. Arnie was glaring at her, but she had yet to let him win the stare down. She sat there with her head high on top of a perfectly straight spine and she radiated determination. Arnie might not know it, but if he wasn't careful, Claire might whip off her bra and go for his throat. Damn, but she was beautiful.

G.T. just about slid out of his chair and under the table when she continued, "Now, I'm sorry, but since we weren't expecting you and there are things I need to discuss with G.T., I'll have to ask you to finish up and leave. You can eat your brownie in your car."

"Nobody eats in my car, not even me. You know that."

She only shrugged. "Fine. I'll put it in a plastic bag and you can take it home. Eat it there. I really don't care."

G.T. figured that was probably the first time anything female had said such a thing to his brother.

Arnie gave him a suspicious look. "What's so darn important and private that you two can't talk about it with me here?" he asked.

G.T. returned a bland smile. Personally he had no clue, but he wasn't about to admit that.

Arnie shoved himself to his feet. "Okay, fine. I know when I'm not wanted. But I meant what I said. I intend to spend more time with the girls."

"I have no problem with that. You are their father, after all."

"Damn right."

"But you'll have to call first and make sure it's convenient. No more just showing up at my front door."

"That's ridiculous. You never have any plans. Why should I—"

"All that's about to change. Some of the people in my night class want to get together now and then, and my law professor has asked me out on a date—"

"He what?" both men roared simultaneously.

Claire continued, acting as though there'd been no outburst. "I told him I didn't think it was professional for a student to date her professor." She watched both men sink back down into their seats.

"I should think not," G.T. muttered.

Then she dropped her bomb. "Of course, the semester only lasts another few weeks. I told him come the first of the year we might be able to work something out."

G.T. put his hand over his eyes and Arnie began to lecture. "He won't marry you, Claire. What with the way you're dressing these days, it's hardly surprising the man would get the wrong impression, but make no mistake, he's only out for what he can get."

She arched her brow. "You've never met the guy and you can tell?" She shrugged. "Not that you aren't right—he is a man, after all." She turned to G.T. and explained, "None of you seem to know what you really want. You have to be led."

She sounded so knowledgeable, so cool, that if the situation hadn't been so serious he would have laughed out loud at the way she was handling Arnie. But then he realized she'd lumped him into the same category and entertained several unworthy suspicions as to what he might be being led to.

She rose from her place. "I'll go pack your brownie now, Arnie. Live it up and eat it in your car. I guess that's about as exciting as things are going to get for you tonight, unless you call Suzanne and apologize for whatever it was you did."

"What makes you think I was at fault? Suzanne's the one—"

But Claire ruthlessly and surprisingly cut him off. "You forget, Arnie. I know you. Of course you're the one at fault. Girls, say good-night to Daddy."

G.T. cleared the table while Claire saw Arnie to the door. She'd had a rocky start, but had ended the evening like an Amazon queen. He didn't know what to think, he realized as he stacked dishes in the sink. It had been great to watch her set Arnie straight, but where was the soft woman, the vulnerable lady, he'd initially set out to protect from the cold, cruel world? It was very possible that Claire no longer needed him.

He brought the milk and pan of brownies back out to the dining room table with him. After refilling the girls' cups and slicing them each a slab of brownie, he sat and waited.

She came back and sat without saying a word. Obviously she had herself under tight control. He poured her some milk and handed her a four-by-four-inch chunk of dessert.

"Thank you," she said.

"You're welcome."

She glanced around, her back still ramrod straight. She'd yet to pick anything up. "The milk container shouldn't be on the table," she announced to the table at large. "It's tacky. Neither should a baking pan. And you should all have plates under your brownies."

"Claire?"

"What?" It came out a little too stridently.

"He's gone, honey."

"We should all have plates. And—"

"The milk container is tacky," he finished for her, giving up for the moment. She was spaced. "I'll put it out in the kitchen, but if anybody wants a refill you're the one who has to go get it."

She nodded. "Fine."

"Will napkins work instead of getting more plates dirty? You don't need to create more work for yourself just to impress me, do you?"

"I'm not trying to impress anybody," she snapped. "Plates are more civilized, that's all. But I guess napkins would be okay this once."

Might as well forego the plates if they represented refinement, he seconded silently. She obviously wasn't feeling terribly civilized right then. Neither was he, come to think of it. Had Arnie found the parking ticket? Had he figured out who'd written it? Man, the you-know-what was going to hit the fan if he turned that bit of information over to his mother. Maybe he'd hire Claire to defend him. Temporary insanity might be a valid plea.

He stuck the milk back in the fridge and grabbed the napkin holder from the cabinet top. "Okay, guys, lift up your brownies while I slide one of these babies underneath," he said as he came back into the room.

"That's okay, Uncle G.T., I don't need one anymore. I'm all done."

"Me, too," Chrissie chirped.

G.T. looked at their chocolate-smeared hands and pixie faces. Maybe he'd talk to Claire about foregoing the frosting next time. The slight loss of flavor would be made up in the more civilized cleanup. Tonight was not the time to say anything, though. Definitely not tonight. He liked his head right where it was. "Well, okay, but both of you head straight for the bathroom and don't let your grimy little mitts touch anything on the way. If the door's shut, call me. Don't touch even the doorknob. Got it? Wash your hands, then start the tub. I'll be right there. Don't get in without me there to lifeguard."

"Don't worry, we won't drowned. We taked swimming lessons last summer," Chrissie cheerfully informed him.

"You never know. You can get all ready, but you can't get in till I'm there, you hear me?"

"Okay," they both agreed and took off down the hall, hands dramatically held straight out in front of them.

Rather cynically, he wondered how long that would last.

"G.T.?"

"Hmm?"

"Why do you do that?"

He reached for his glass of milk and took a healthy swig. He'd need the fortification, somehow he was sure of that. "Do what?"

He was relieved when she finally picked up her brownie and nibbled delicately. Maybe that unnatural shell she'd encased herself in the past little while was cracking.

She swallowed. "Take over like that. You know, clearing the table, serving dessert, getting the girls into the tub."

His eyebrows lowered. Man, she was in a strange mood tonight, for sure. He'd been trying to be helpful—what was that, a crime or something? That one law course she was taking was one too many as far as he was concerned. "I'm sorry if you think I was usurping your role, Claire," he apologized stiffly. "It wasn't my intention." It was also the last time he went out of his way to be nice, too.

"It wasn't stepping on my toes, not exactly. But Arnie would never have done any of those things without my having to ask, probably more than once."

"I am not my brother." And he was damn tired of having to point that out. He heard water running in the distance and had no idea if he should get up and go supervise or not.

Claire moistened her finger and blotted chocolate crumbs off the table before popping them in her mouth. "No, you're not," she agreed seriously. "You're not."

He waited, sensing she wasn't through. But water was still running and the tub was going to end up in the apartment below if he didn't get in there and shut it off. "Claire—"

"I heard from New York today."

Uh-oh. "You did?"

"Yeah." She ran her finger around the top of her milk glass.

He was afraid to ask. "So what'd they say?"

"Well, it was the first time I've ever gotten anything other than a form rejection."

"Uh-huh." What the hell did that mean? The water was still going. He really needed to get in there, but she obviously wanted to get this out, too. You know, loving a woman was tough stuff. He wanted to be there for her, but right now she needed him in two different spots at once. Wait a minute, had he said *loving* her? Well, sure, loving, he guessed. *But* he'd meant it in more of a cosmic sense. One human's love for another of the same species—more the theological definition of love than... the other kind. He breathed a sigh of relief. That was it. He did love her, but cosmically. Yeah. "Listen, honey, I really want to hear this, but I've got to run a check on Frick and Frack in the bathroom. Don't go anywhere. I'll be right back."

"I'll do it," she said, but didn't move.

He got up. "Stay put. I want to hear this."

"It's not important." She sighed to his back. "I mean, they didn't offer to buy it or anything. They just said they'd be willing to take another look if I was willing to do a lot of rewriting, clean it all up."

"Clean what all up?" he called back from his position halfway down the hall. "There weren't any swears in there. I'd know. I've got a very deep vocabulary when it comes to that.

"Okay, you two, turn off the water. Look at this. Another couple of inches and you'd be overflowing. We'll have to let half of this out."

Claire wandered down the hall after him. He almost crashed into her after he'd taken care of things temporarily in the bathroom and had turned around to get back to her.

"Umph, there you are."

"It wasn't swearing, G.T. They objected to the adversarial aspects of pitting a child against a dentist. In a nutshell, I wrote a politically incorrect children's story. How is that possible? I'm an enlightened nineties parent and I've evidently written a story that will turn a kid off going to the dentist for life. I got the definite impression an entire generation will grow up with blackened, rotting teeth if that book goes into print as is."

"Don't be ridiculous." He glowered down at her. "Go ahead and get in, kids. I guess I can watch you from here. Now, Claire—"

"I honestly thought it was *funny* to have a cement truck pull up to the dentist's open window when it was time to fill Maureen's cavity."

"It was," he corroborated loyally.

"No, it was frightening. I have it on the best of authority."

"Bull. Kids know fantasy when they see it. None of them expect a cement truck to appear when they have a cavity filled. It's not like they're growing up when we did. They've all been to the dentist's office by the time they were three, and your story was geared older than that. Stop splashing in there, you guys."

"They liked the characters and they liked my style."

"Well, that's good," he decided judiciously. "I mean it, you two. Quit horsing around."

"She got soap in my eye."

"Did not."

"Did, too!"

"Melissa, dunk your face in the water and rinse the soap off of your face, then both of you behave or I'm not going to let you take any more baths. I'll just take you out in the yard and hose you off with the garden hose."

"Even in the winter?" Chrissie asked, interested.

"Yeah."

"Wow."

"Now behave."

"You realize, of course," Claire began as though debating some philosophical academic issue, "that you've probably scarred my daughters for life with that response."

"I wasn't being politically correct?"

"No."

"So tell me, what should I have said to keep the two little dears from soaping each other's eyes out until they were both blind?"

Claire shrugged and rubbed her forehead. "Darned if I know anymore. I guess I should be reasoning with them, pointing out the benefits to society on this crowded planet of people that can participate in the give and take of daily living without soaping each other's eyes. Perhaps bring out studies of tribes that did versus tribes that did not soap each other's eyes. I could use graph paper to show the decline over the years of the tribes that did and use a different color ink to show the other tribe flourishing."

G.T. stared at her for a moment. "That's really very good. Perhaps you should consider writing adult humor instead of children's books."

Claire walked into the bathroom and sat on the closed toilet seat as she contemplated the activity going on in the tub. G.T. followed her in to lean against the door. An odd room to gather in, Claire was suddenly aware of the intimacy of congregating in the bathroom. She took a breath. "Making their bathtub behavior the standard by which society succeeds or fails might be kind of a heavy burden to lay on a three- and five-year-old," she felt obliged to mention. "Laying guilt on your kids is probably no more politically correct than having their cavities filled by a cement truck."

"Hmm, probably not."

"G.T.," she burst out, "I simply cannot write one of those sappy PC kids' stories where the dentist comes in all happy and smiley and counts the child's teeth. How can they always be amazed that there are twenty? Haven't they figured that much out by the time they get out of school and into private practice? Darn it, everything's ruined if I have to take out the cement truck."

G.T. eyed her nervously. "Okay, calm down now. I'll help you get the kids into pajamas, and when they're down we'll figure this out."

She stood and reached for a bath towel. "No, when they're down, I want you to teach me how to throw a guy. You never did, you know, and tonight I'm in the mood to throw somebody. Might as well be you.

"Come on, you two. Out of the tub."

G.T. looked first at her, then blankly at the towel she'd thrust into his hands. She really was going to make him crazy. She felt like throwing somebody around so he should volunteer? What did *that* say about their relationship? He wasn't so sure he loved her right then, not even cosmically. "Why in God's name do you want me to teach you how to throw somebody now? That guy hasn't been back, has he?"

Briskly she ran the terry cloth over her youngest daughter's squirming body, then tackled her hair. "Hold still, pumpkin," she said. "No, no more burglars, at least not in this building. I just think that society being what it is—"

"Everybody soaping each other's eyes?" he questioned dryly.

"Something like that," she agreed and spread her arms. "After all, if I'm going to have to start dating again, I might need to defend myself. I already told you that." She picked up the towel from where she'd left it draped over Chrissie's head and began rubbing again.

"Yeah," he admitted glumly. She had. And the idea of her dating, let alone having to defend her virtue without him there to lend a helping hand, really offended him. He hated the idea of anybody touching her even casually. Heck, the whole reason he'd put off teaching her a few tricks of the trade was because he knew what coming in contact with her did to his nerve endings. Any other male just running into her for the first time would probably be knocked flat on his back. What made it all worse, he thought with a grimace, is that they'd probably be slick enough operators to hang on to her when they fell, pulling her down on top of them, and she'd fall for it because she hadn't played any dating games for so long. His eyes narrowed into slits. "Okay, I'll show you a few tricks."

"You will?"

"I just said I would, didn't I?" Of course, his own nerves would be shot to hell and back by the time they were done, but, hey, think nothing of it. All in the line of duty, don't you know.

"Well, if you're going to be put out, we don't have to do it."

"It's not going to put me out." Not much. "Let's just get the two munchkins into bed, and then we'll do it," Oh, God, don't even *think* along those lines. "All right?"

It took them forty-five minutes and a new Toaster Beady and Maureen Schneider—this one involving going to the doctor's for booster shots. G.T. was positive the editor in New York would be appalled at the size needle this particular M.D. used on innocent little five-year-olds. He'd paled a bit himself when he heard the nurse needed a crane to support the syringe. But shortly after Toaster and Maureen eventually prevailed, giving the doctor the shot instead much to the little ones delight, Melissa and Chrissie were tucked in and the light flipped off.

He and Claire retreated to the living room. He was as ready as he'd ever be.

"Okay," Claire said. "All's quiet on the western front, so what do we do?"

Put your arms up here, around my neck, he longed to say. Let your fingertips play a bit in the hair at the nape. Meanwhile, I'll strum your spine like a fine bass fiddle. I'm such a guy I'll even let you pull your blouse over your head and off so I can make sure I'm hitting each fret exactly right. He sighed. In only his highest-caliber dreams. "Turn around and pretend you're out walking."

"Walking?"

"Yeah. I'll come up from behind and grab you." Lordy, lordy, just what he'd been trying to avoid these past few weeks.

"Oh, okay." Claire pivoted and used her hips to sashay away. "Like this?"

His eyes bugged out. No, not like that. Good grief, if she'd taken to walking like that, no wonder she expected to be dating soon. Any male in a ten-mile radius with better than twenty-two-hundred vision would be following after her, panting and clutching at his chest. Damn, forget the self-defense. She needed to get her CPR certificate updated instead. He thumped his own chest, trying to steady his heart's beat. "Just walk normally, okay?"

"This is how I walk," she protested.

"No, it's not. I would have noticed."

"Probably you've just never followed me before."

She had him there. "Never mind. Turn back around. Here I come." God, he hoped not. If he could just hold off until he got back to his own place, he could spend an hour or two under a cold shower. There was a slim chance he'd be back under control after that. He hooked an arm around her neck and tugged her back against his chest. Make that three hours in the cold shower. "Be real nice to me, pretty lady," he growled. "And I'll let you walk away when I'm done."

"My, the dating world really *has* changed, hasn't it?"

"Claire, if you're not going to be serious about this..." he started to warn. This was about the greatest corporal work of mercy he'd ever performed. She damn well better be learning something here. Personally he was dying.

"I will, I will. I'm sorry. Okay, tell me what to do."

"Try to get away," he instructed and braced himself.

Claire pulled on his arm to no avail and tried to get an elbow into his ribs, but he had her right up against him and she couldn't get the leverage she needed. Then she thought of stomping on his foot, but all that produced was a grunt. G.T. was too close for her to think properly, and he was cheating, too. It was his aftershave that was doing her in, she decided. Probably had an alcohol base. She had no head for alcohol and G.T. knew that. Claire was breathing heavily by the time she panted, "All right, I give."

He wished. "You've got to act fast. I'd have had you in an alley by now, doing whatever I wanted. Now put your hand over mine and don't pry at it, hold it to you while you take one step out and back with your right foot. Dip while you're doing it."

She did as instructed. "Like this?"

"Yeah. Duck your head out from under my arm and you're free. Now you run like hell."

"Is that all?" she complained. "I want to deck you."

"You are not going to stick around long enough to deck me. You are going to get out of here as fast as your little legs will carry you." Good advice. Perhaps he ought to heed it himself since Claire obviously wasn't. "Head for a lighted house or store. Someplace where there are people."

She looked ready to argue further.

"Just do it. And if somebody throws you, stay down and spin on your spine like your legs are the needle of a compass and your mugger is true north, got it? Then kick like hell whenever the jerk tries to get near enough to follow you down."

"I don't know, G.T. I suppose this stuff is good to learn, but it doesn't seem like the kind of thing that would arise in a date situation."

He didn't know about that. With that new walk of hers, she'd probably attract a lot of the Neanderthal primitive-mind types. Who knew if they'd try to throw her over their shoulder and take her home to their cave? "So what do you suggest?"

"I just think maybe we should practice more datelike stuff."

There went his heart again, back up into his throat. She was killing him by inches tonight. "All right. Sit over here next to me. We'll pretend we're at a singles' bar and I'm bothering you."

"G.T., I'd never go to a singles' bar."

No. No, she wouldn't. She wasn't that type. "Okay, all right. We'll, ah—"

"I know. We'll put on some slow music. We can dance and you can show me how to fend off whatever moves guys are putting on their dates on the dance floor these days."

That did it. She was talking stroke territory now. "Listen, Claire, honey—"

But she was already pulling out tapes. "Here's one that would work. Johnny Mathis retrospective. My mom bought this for me, oh, probably five years ago, at least. It might have been my first wedding anniversary, now that I think about it. She said my father and her used to make out on the dance floor while Johnny crooned in the background. Frankly I can't picture those two engaging in anything so tasteless, but then again I guess everybody has a difficult time imagining their parents as sexual people, don't you think? And—"

The woman was rambling, G.T. thought. And look at her fumbling the tape as she tried to slip it into the player. Why, she was as nervous as he was. Perhaps she'd lost interest in the evening's self-defense instruction. "Claire—"

"What?" She pounced eagerly on his interruption and he knew she'd realized she was running on.

"Push the play button."

Mutely she did.

"Now come here."

Claire crossed the room to stand before him. Anxiety played over her expressive face. "G.T.—"

He gathered her into his arms as an ancient Johnny Mathis song wrapped itself around them like fine satin. "Shh." He began to sway and she followed his movements easily. "You wanted to know what kind of moves to expect on the dance floor, so hush up and start taking notes. I've been told I've got some good ones."

Her eyes narrowed and she peered up at him suspiciously. "Oh, yeah? By whom?"

G.T. chuckled quietly and refused to answer. Taking her arms, he looped them around his neck. Then, gently, he pushed her head onto his shoulder and savored the feel of her. God, it was good. How *any* man could have walked away from this was beyond him. As for himself, he was drowning in her womanliness and his only regret was that, like Nathan Hale, he was sorry he had but one life to give up here tonight.

He bussed her neck with his lips and felt the delightful shiver that took her. Ah, yes, he thought as he snuggled right up against her, Mrs. Salem had tried every trick in the book to make the American Revolution come alive when G.T. had been a bored but cool seventh grader. But he had to admit, none of her ploys had made him feel this kind of kinship to an historical figure.

He rubbed his cheek against her hair, releasing the floral scent of her shampoo trapped there. He breathed deeply. Yes, indeed. Nate, my man, you had the right of it.

Claire felt his hands begin to move on her spine. Her whole back tingled. "G.T.?" she murmured questioningly.

"Hmm?"

"Do I do anything to you yet?"

"No, not yet."

"Oh." He sighed into her hair and a small shudder took her. "You'll let me know?"

"Yeah," he agreed, his voice sounding slightly slurred. "No problem."

"Good." Until then, she guessed she could just relax and enjoy. And that, my friends, would not be too difficult to do. G.T.'s arms were strong and solid around her. His heart beat rhythmically beneath her ear and she was feeling very, very mellow. Like one glass of wine too many, only she hadn't had anything to drink.

Johnny slid smoothly from one ballad into the next. When G.T. led them past one end table, she reached out and switched off that light. "The glare was bothering me," she explained when he leaned back and looked down at her.

He didn't argue, just tucked her head back onto his shoulder and said, "Hmm." She could hear it rumble around in his chest beneath her ear. It sounded self-satisfied, but tonight she didn't care. She wanted this one perfect evening for her internal memory book.

G.T. slid his hands around to her sides and ran them up and down a bit.

She made no protest.

He kissed her neck, nibbled a bit on the exposed earlobe and used his tongue, hot and wet, inside the pink shell of her ear.

This time she murmured something into his chest, but she still didn't object. No, she lifted her face to his and kissed him. It was sweet and naively passionate and it just about knocked him on his *keister*. "Come on, honey, let's sit this next one out." And he guided her to the sofa.

She made a token protest as he arranged their bodies on the couch. "I don't know, G.T., do you think this is very smart?"

"No, probably not," he admitted, "but I do think it's probably necessary."

She'd never been necessary before and found she rather liked the idea. "Necessary, huh?" she asked as he crowded her corner of the sofa.

"Yeah," he growled and lowered his mouth over hers.

She let her fingers play in the hair at the nape of his neck while his teeth nibbled at her bottom lip. There wasn't even a token protest when his hand moved to her breast. It felt too good, warm and right. His hand belonged there and she belonged with him. Maybe she didn't need his protection anymore, but they needed each other in other ways and he recognized it was not a one-way need, may never have been. He needed her, too.

Beginning to writhe, Claire undid several of his shirt buttons and slid her hand inside. His chest hair was crisp and springy, his male nipple, flat and hard. Lord, she wanted this man.

She felt him freeing her blouse from the top of her skirt. She wondered, hoped, he was going to touch her more intimately. Encouragingly she kissed his shoulder, then carefully tested the muscles there with her teeth.

He growled and she smiled with delight. Teeth were exciting. Odd she'd never realized that before. Why teeth could be— She sat up with a start. "Oh my gosh."

G.T. sank back into the sofa, holding his nose. "Ow! For crying out loud, Claire, what just got into you? What's wrong?"

She turned and stared at him. "I just thought of how I could redo Toaster Beady's and Maureen Schneider's trip to the dentist. You know, make it politically correct but still maintain the integrity of their characters."

Chapter Ten

G.T. rested his head on the sofa back, closed his eyes momentarily and rubbed the nose he was sure Claire had just broken when she'd smashed her head into it by sitting up. Was it even possible that while he'd been thoroughly involved in and enjoying the proceedings at hand, his lovemaking had reminded Claire of a dental procedure?

He was losing his touch.

No, it was her. Had to be. The woman was a menace. He desperately wanted to roll his eyes in response to the predicament he currently found himself in, but his nose hurt too badly to concentrate long enough to pull the feat off. He felt her hand on his shoulder.

"Hey. G.T.? Are you all right?"

No, he was not all right, what did she think? She'd just dislocated half his face, for crying out loud! "Yeah, no problem. I'm fine." If only the stars on the backs of his eyelids would go away, he'd be even better.

"I didn't mean to hurt you."

"I know."

"I just had this blinding realization right in the middle of... things," she finished lamely.

"I noticed." And he didn't want to talk about it, either.

She knelt on the sofa cushion beside him. "Here, take your hand away from your face and let me take a look. Your voice sounds funny. Kind of nasally. It's not bleeding, is it?"

"I don't think so. Claire, stop pulling on my hand. I can't take it away just yet." His nose might fall off if he did.

"Well, at least open your eyes and let me check that your pupils are dilated evenly."

"I don't have a concussion."

"How do you know? Just let me look."

"In a minute."

She exhaled so loudly he could hear it. "You're being extremely difficult, G.T."

He was being difficult? *He* was? "I'm not the one thinking about the dentist in the middle of lovemaking."

Claire sat back and crossed her arms over her chest. "We weren't making love."

"Sure felt like it to me."

"It did? Well, I mean, it may have *felt* that way, but—"

He sighed. "Never mind, honey. You're obviously not ready to discuss what happens between us whenever we're together." Truthfully, neither was he. Cautiously he removed his hand from his face and opened his eyes. There. The stars were receding and his ears had stopped ringing. "Tell me about Toaster and Maureen's trip to the dentist instead. It seems to be uppermost on your mind."

"You sure you want to hear this?"

Man, talk about naive. Here she'd just gravely insulted his manhood, did she even have to ask? Evidently so. Anyone else would know he was merely being polite. "Yes, I'm sure."

She leaned forward eagerly. "Well, while I was, uh, nibbling on your shoulder a minute ago—"

Oh, please. Don't remind him. His body was just starting to relax. "Biting," he corrected firmly. "It wasn't a nibble, it was a bite."

She looked at him unsurely.

"Felt great, too."

Claire was evidently not at ease with this type of intimate discussion. She turned an interesting shade of pink and rushed to gloss over his interruption. "Yes, well, whatever. While I was... doing that, I had this sudden flash of inspiration."

There she went, reminding him again of his failure to keep her properly focused. "Toaster and Maureen?" he prompted.

"Right. Toaster and Maureen. Here's what I was thinking they could do."

G.T. listened, allowing his body to wind down along with Claire's storyline. "Cute," he finally proclaimed it. "Why don't you give those rotten, no-good editors another chance with this new idea?"

"They're not rotten," she immediately protested.

"Ah, our perception has changed now that the door's been opened a crack, hmm?"

Claire hemmed and hawed a bit over that. "Well, sort of," she finally admitted. "I mean, I guess they're okay."

G.T. had draped his arm along the back of the sofa now that he no longer needed his hand to hold his nose on. Claire sat back against his side and he wondered if she was conscious of the way she'd snuggled up against him. He certainly was. He let his arm drop onto her shoulder and lightly kneaded the muscle there. She felt right there, he was sorry to say.

He was debating how to tell her about the feelings for her he was unwillingly beginning to recognize when she spoke.

"G.T.?"

"Yeah?"

"I really hate torts."

His hand stilled as he tried to follow her line of reasoning. "I beg your pardon?"

"Torts. You know, the law class I'm taking. I hate it."

"Oh, well, the semester's almost over. In just a few short weeks you'll be on to something else," he encouraged bracingly. "Legal procedure or contracts."

There was a brief pause, then Claire said, "They sound almost as dry as torts."

He thought about that. "They do, don't they?"

She reached up to the hand on her shoulder and twined her fingers into his. He squeezed reassuringly.

"The thing is, I'm no longer so sure I'm cut out to be a lawyer."

He could have told her that back when she'd first come up with this harebrained idea. Oh, well, better late than never. If she was finally going to come out from her divorce-induced trauma, maybe now *was* the time to start exploring the possibility of a future together. He could test the waters a bit, at any rate. "Claire—"

"But I can't quit."

That stopped him. "Why the hell not?"

"Everybody would think I was a failure. A quitter."

"No, they wouldn't." They'd just think she'd come to her senses.

"Yes, they would," she insisted.

He put his head back and used his free hand to rub his eyes. How was it that every time he thought he was actually getting a handle on his life it took another right-angle turn? "I, for one, will not consider you a quitter. I, along with most of the population not currently in law school, recognize that there is a glut of lawyers on the market right now. You could go through all those classes and still be jobless when you come out. Oakley is not exactly Harvard or Yale, you know, and that's where most of the hires will be."

But Claire wasn't really listening. She was too wrapped up in her own reasoning process, such as it was. "I could do it, you know," she said. "It's not that I can't handle it."

"But you don't like it."

She sighed. "Not liking I could deal with. I'm past that and into active hating."

"So quit."

"And do what?"

He threw up his free hand. "Write politically correct children's stories, I don't know!"

"But don't you see? Law has prestige. It infers competence and intelligence, all the things that writing kiddie books doesn't. They make me soft, pink. I don't know, fuzzy."

Yes, all the things she was when she wasn't off the wall. "You can be intelligent and fuzzy at the same time."

"Arnie wouldn't respect it."

Ah, so that was it. He closed his eyes briefly. Damn. "Why do you care what Arnie thinks?"

He felt her shrug helplessly.

"I don't know why, I just do."

In other words, she wasn't over him yet.

"I want him to see what he gave up. I want him to be sorry."

Afraid to ask, afraid not to, he questioned, "Would you take him back?"

"No, of course not. I don't think."

Terrific. He disengaged his hand from hers and stood to face her.

She looked up at him, confusion mirrored in her eyes. "G.T., I'm twenty-seven years old. How come I still don't know what I want to be when I grow up?"

He shook his head. "I don't know, honey. But I'll admit I'm a little confused myself." Everything that had been so clear only a little while ago was back shrouded in fog. What should she do? What should *he* do? What was the meaning of life? "I guess I'll go on home. I need to do some serious decision making myself."

She used the hand he extended to pull herself up. "What are you trying to decide?"

Nothing too shattering, just the whole rest of his life. He raked a hand through his hair. "It's time I figured out where I'm heading, too, sweetness. I've never been much for books, yet here I am back in school myself. Why? Probably to buy respect with a college degree."

"You're plenty smart enough to get a degree," she said.

"Yeah, I know. So why do I feel like I have to prove it? I don't like book learning, I'm much better with hands-on kinds of stuff."

"So why are you doing it? It's got to be hard to work all day and then go to school at night."

She walked with him to the door where he stopped and gazed down at her. "I've been feeling itchy lately at work. Restless. But when push comes to shove, you know what?"

"What?"

He leaned against the front door frame, a faintly surprised expression on his face. Then he nodded his head. "I've never really thought of it in this light before, but I'm going to really be ticked if it turns out I'm sweating it out to get this stinking degree to prove to my mother and Arnie that I'm as good as he is."

Claire looked thoughtful. "You know, in his own way, Arnie really did a number on both of us."

"We let him," G.T. reflected, still standing in the open front doorway.

"So we're halfway to blame? I'll have to think about that one."

"Yeah, me, too."

"G.T.?"

"Yes?"

She reached up and looped her arms around his neck. Standing on tiptoes, she kissed him, her lips lingering lightly like a butterfly having trouble with a stubborn flower blossom.

When she began to withdraw, G.T. used his hand to cradle her head. "I don't think it's properly pollinated yet," he murmured against her lips as he held her head in place.

"What?"

"And I think you may have missed some of the nectar, too."

"G.T., you're not making any sense."

He was to him. He definitely was to him.

"Will you call me?" she asked a bit breathlessly when he finally released her mouth.

"You mean when I get home?"

"No. When you're done deciding."

So she recognized there was more being decided here than career choices. Well, he'd known she wasn't stupid. He touched the back of a finger to her cheek. "We'll see, doll face. We'll see." Then he got himself out of there while he still had the strength to leave.

He was supposed to work a double shift the next day and he knew he needed to sleep. He stripped to his shorts in preparation for bed. But instead, he paced. Back and forth, up and down. Through the living room and dinette at a forty-five-degree angle to maximize the distance he covered.

He'd known for months he was interested in Claire, but he'd hung back, waiting for her to recover from her divorce, waiting for the soft woman he'd known in the early years of her marriage to return so he could claim her.

"Time to face up to the very real possibility that he might wait till hell froze over for the soft, fuzzy Claire to return. She could well be gone forever." And just how well would he deal with a brassy blond wife who wore red miniskirts with stridently yellow poet blouses? he asked himself.

"I don't know." He groaned. "I just don't know." He pivoted and started back across the living room. "And I really need to go to bed." But to what point, when he knew he was so far from sleep that if he crawled in right then it could well be the middle of the following week before he drifted off?

It was his own motivation that was really bothering him, he decided as he crossed into the eating area. Why had he gotten interested in Claire in the first place? She deserved somebody who came to her with straightforward intentions. Somebody who wanted her because they wanted her. His reasoning was such a tangled skein of motives, it might well take a Ph.D. in psychology a month of Sundays to unravel them. And by then, he'd be flat broke from paying the fee and too poor to marry her even if he wanted to.

Was it because his brother had picked her and he always tried—and failed—to outdo his brother? Sick, really sick. Besides, he thought he'd gotten over that in adolescence.

Maybe it was the role he played in his family. The Responsible One. He'd always felt obliged to clean up the messes big brother made and walked away from. What did that make G.T.? Some kind of masochistic martyr? And Claire would hardly view his marrying her as a corporal work of mercy in a charitable light. She'd probably strangle him with her brassiere, and he'd deserve it.

"Maybe I'm rebelling," he told himself, not liking the last alternative at all. "That could be it." Maybe it hadn't been enough when he'd had his high school's initials carved into his hair and gone shirtless to the big end-of-the-year early-November football game. He'd thought about going to prom that year wearing purple high-top sneakers to match his cummerbund and his date's dress. "I should have done it," he lamented out loud. Maybe if he had, he wouldn't now be feeling the need to compete with his brother, if in fact, that was what he was feeling. "It's just so juvenile," he complained to the empty room. "That can't be it," and he waved his hand in the room, erasing the possibility.

You know, it would just be too gross if it all came down to the fact that he was finally pursuing his degree and Claire to prove to his family that he was as good as their firstborn.

Damn it, why was he back in school? Why was he so captivated by a wild woman with dyed hair? He covered the distance between the living room and dinette a few more times, finally throwing up his hands in aggravation. "I can't stand it. I'm going to bed before my reaction time is shot to hell. If my being a zombie ends up with some hood getting the drop on me tomorrow, that'll really frost my cake." Would Claire water his grave with her tears? he wondered. Did she care? Man, he was going nuts.

He crawled into bed in his darkened bedroom, lying back flat on his back, and laced his hands behind his head. He stared at the ceiling for what remained of the night. Unfortunately he found no answers written up there, either.

Somehow he managed to get through the next twenty-four hours without getting himself shot, but when he dragged himself back to his apartment and determinedly closed his eyes...nothing. No sandman. Hell, he couldn't even pull off a decent yawn.

"This is ridiculous," he finally announced to the empty room. "Even the bogeyman who used to hide under my bed until I was asleep so he could come get me when I was a kid has probably given up on me tonight," he groused.

He wondered how Claire was doing. Had she wrestled her private demons into submission? Her roots had been showing last time he'd seen her. Would she redye her beautiful brown hair for her law professor? Indenture her soul to the beautician for a can of mousse?

Would she finish law school to prove a point to her ex or quit and write politically correct children's stories?

G.T. felt trapped in a bad soap opera as he contemplated the various conundrums that had ensnared him lately. What the devil was going on?

He probably ought to just stay away from Claire. The woman clouded his thinking processes.

He'd encouraged her to give up law and write. What if she did? How would he feel about that? If he was in this to prove something to his family—not that he was convinced of that—a lot of the prestige gained in the relationship would be lost.

"Who says she'd marry me, anyway?" he asked out loud. They'd never really discussed it. He could very well be going through this whole ridiculous process of trying to identify his motives, making sure he'd be marrying her for the right reasons—he certainly didn't want to deal her any more emotional harm than his family was already responsible for—only to have her tell him to drop dead, she had the hots for the torts professor.

This entire situation was making him crazy. Fact was, if he'd been a drinking man, the owner of the liquor store two blocks down would be plunking down a deposit on a new luxury car about now. On that happy note, he stripped out of his uniform and flung himself down on his bed to grimly study his ceiling for another endless night.

"Hey, man, far be it from me to point out the obvious, but you look bad," his partner informed him as they came off duty the following afternoon. "You coming down with the flu or something?"

He wished it was that easy. Flu he'd be over by the end of the week. This? Who knew. G.T. stretched as he stepped out of the squad, trying to work some of the kinks out of his back. "Naw, nothing like that. Just been having trouble sleeping the past couple of nights, that's all."

"Ah." His partner nodded wisely. "Women trouble, huh? Listen, I've got the perfect cure. What do you say we go down to Teddy's over on Morse Avenue? He's got a big screen TV in there and we can watch the Bulls game while we down a few."

"Can't," G.T. said succinctly.

"Oh, come on. Why not?"

"Gotta go to class. I'm learning how to be an *effective communicator*."

"Give it up." His partner grunted. "For you, that would be a lost cause."

It very probably was. G.T. sighed as they walked up the steps into the station. Hell, he was still having trouble getting the left side of his brain to speak to the right side. He was still clueless as how to proceed in this relationship, if you could call it that, with Claire.

Why worry about the rest of the world under those circumstances?

"Still think you'd have a better time at the bar," G.T.'s partner advised. "And I bet we could talk MacKenzie and Lytle into going with us."

"You're probably right," G.T. agreed, "but I gotta get some sleep. English class is my best bet right now. Ten minutes into the prof's lecture I'll be sawing boards."

"Be easier if you just took whatever lady is in question here to bed."

No, it wouldn't. It would make things infinitely messier, he was sure.

He still felt that way as he picked his way through rush-hour traffic on his way out to Oakley that night. In fact, the longer he stayed away from Claire and the temptation she represented, the clearer he could see that ending things before they really got started was the right thing to do here. He wanted her on many different levels, not all of them admirable. He refused to use her in a less than honorable manner; therefore, he would stay away. Being innately the noble soul he was, he would leave the way open for her to find love with somebody else, some altruistic jerk he would hate on sight.

He guided the car effortlessly into a slot in one of the Oakley lots as he reached that decision. He turned off the engine and rested his head on the steering wheel. All that thinking had given him a headache. He was quitting school, quitting the force. He'd go to Tibet and be a monk. Right after class. Provided his headache let up.

G.T. dragged himself out of the car and into the building. He slouched in his seat and tried to focus on the front of the room.

You know, there was a good chance he could have figured out all by himself that one ought to limit the use of the word "very" in one's writing. And, yep, it probably was a good idea to use complete sentences when composing a term paper.

Come on, man, let's get to the exciting stuff. What about *footnotes?* Now they were hot.

He needed to go see Claire. Not long enough to lose his resolve, but just spend enough time to explain things. He owed her that. After all, she'd asked him to let her know when he'd made his decision and it would be rude to just suddenly stop showing up with no explanations.

Besides, he was interested—on an intellectual level, of course—to learn what she'd decided to do, as well.

Well, if he didn't catch her on break, he'd stop in at the apartment tomorrow.

He nodded his head. Uh-huh, uh-huh, *adjectives.* Wow, things were getting very, strike that, extremely heavy-duty here, he'd best pay attention so he wouldn't miss out.

"G.T.?"

"Yep, in the flesh."

Claire closed the door, loosened the chain guard, then opened the door wide. She got her first good look at him. "You don't look so good, G.T. Have you been sick or something?"

G.T. grimaced. "No, I have not been sick. Thank you for asking."

"Well, then, have you been putting in a lot of hours? Something's got you looking haggard, that's for sure."

He rolled his eyes; he couldn't help it. "Look, are you going to let me in, or are we going to stand out in the hallway discussing the erosion of my appearance?"

She stepped aside. "Oh, sorry."

He nodded his head curtly in acknowledgment as he came into the apartment. Man, lose a little sleep and you'd think he'd aged twenty years. He hadn't thought he looked *that* bad. "You don't look too hot yourself, toots. So what's your excuse?" he asked as he stalked into the living room.

Self-consciously she combed her hair with her fingers. "Nothing's wrong with me. I've just had a little trouble sleeping, that's all."

That made two of them. He threw himself onto her sofa after eyeing it evilly. Things were not getting off to a good start here. He took a deep breath, determined to start fresh. G.T. propped one ankle up on its opposing knee and bobbed his foot impatiently up and down off the end. "I'm sorry to hear you aren't sleeping well," he tried. There, how was that for polite? "What do you suppose the trouble might be?"

She looked at him in surprise. "Don't you remember? We were both deciding what we were going to do with the rest of our lives."

"Oh, that."

"G.T.," Claire said in a warning way.

"Just kidding, honey. I haven't done anything *but* think about the rest of my life since I last saw you." And it seemed to him it stretched out before him in a singularly empty and lonely straight line.

"What did you decide?" Claire asked, her voice sounding tentative to his ears.

"Tell me what you decided first."

She perched on the chair across from him and leaned forward. "I'm going to quit school at the end of the semester," she informed him. "My parents always put such value on education that it was a really hard decision, but that's what I'm going to do. I've thought and thought about this, and even if my writing doesn't pan out, I still don't want to study law. I don't need to prove anything to anybody. I'm done apologizing for who and what I am. I'll find something else I genuinely like to do if I can't write."

It sounded as if she was finally finding herself again, G.T. realized. That was good—he guessed. But now he was sadder than ever at being left out in the cold.

"That's great, honey. I'm happy for you." Sort of.

He realized she was looking at him expectantly. "Oh, you want to know what I decided? I'm going to finish up the semester, too, and then I'm quitting. I've decided to opt out of the sibling competition for good." He shrugged. "I'll get over whatever it is that's been making me feel so itchy sooner or later. Police work's pretty decent most of the time and I'm good at it."

G.T.'s foot bobbing picked up tempo considerably as he came to the hard part. The guys down at the station would fall down laughing if they could see him now, he told himself. The foot bobbing wasn't burning enough of his energy off and he ended up jumping off the sofa and pacing the floor. He looked down the darkened hallway. "Where are the kids?" he asked when he finally realized how quiet it was in the apartment.

"Your mom's got them. She said she's tired of being understanding, and no matter what you come up with she's not taking any more vacations, cruises, or visiting any more long-lost relatives. She said she's given us enough time to get our acts together, and she missed her grandchildren, and to heck with us. She also says she has a few words to say to you about a certain parking ticket."

G.T. had to laugh. "Sounds like Mom all right."

Claire eyed him as he paced back across the room. "G.T., I wouldn't have twisted the building manager's arm to redo my floors if I'd known you were going to be like this. If you don't settle down, you're going to scratch them all up again."

"Sorry."

"Come on, something's still bugging you. Out with it."

Okay. So here went nothing. "Claire, I've been thinking through a lot more than just a simple career choice. That choice has a lot to do with where my relationship, if you could call it that, with you was headed." He looked at her impatiently. "Let's be real here. You had to know I was hanging around for more reasons than just the fact that I felt sorry for you after Arnie's rough treatment and wanted to help you out. I mean, I *did* feel bad about the way Arnie handled the divorce and I *did* want to help you out, but on another level, I wanted you for myself, you see?"

He paused in what he knew was a confusing dissertation and asked, "Wouldn't it have been a gas to thumb our noses at Arnie if we'd gotten together, especially if we'd both become lawyers—or maybe you could have been a lawyer and me a doctor—and we'd outearned Arnie four to one or something like that?

Anyway, what I'm saying is that all these different needs operating on different levels would interfere with the only level that counts, the one where I need you for yourself, not the ones that allow me to play hero or savior or jealous sibling or—"

"I get the idea."

"Well, to make a long story short, I decided you needed somebody who'd come to you without all that emotional baggage."

"You decided?"

"Yes, and what I really came by to tell you tonight is that I won't be stopping by much anymore," G.T. told her heroically. "I'll miss you and the girls, but you need your life back so you can get on with it."

Claire jumped out of her chair and put her hands on her hips. She stood nose to nose with him. "Well, aren't you Mr. Nobility," she retorted.

"Listen, honey, I'm only trying to do what's best—"

"Who asked you to? Where do you get off making decisions all by yourself that affect us both?"

His brow rose. "I—"

"Oh, just be quiet. I've got a few pithy thoughts of my own to add to this heretofore one-sided conversation."

"Did you talk to Arnie like this?"

"No, and I see now it was a serious mistake that I don't intend to make twice."

"Oh."

"Exactly. Now listen up, Jack. *Everybody* operates on more than one level. Nobody's going to knock on my door to offer me their pure unencumbered heart on a silver platter. We've all got baggage we're carrying around. I operate on more than one level myself." She poked him in the chest. "I'm glad you finally brought this up—I've been waiting, you know. Now that it's out in the open, let me say that I know a relationship with me would fill more than one need in you and I don't care."

He was amazed. "You don't?"

"No." She poked him in the chest again. "I don't. Because guess what? My relationship with *you* would fill a lot of needs for me, too."

"Like what?" he asked suspiciously. This was ridiculous. Claire was not a user, not like him.

"I wouldn't be lonely at night anymore—or scared."

"You could put away the attack bra," he murmured to himself.

"Probably not. I'm sure I'll want to keep it handy to use on you when you're making me crazy like you are right now."

"Sorry." But he wasn't, not really.

"You'll be stuck with an unimpressive wife who writes children's stories—and they may not all be politically correct—instead of a fancy, shmancy ladylawyer wife," she warned. "There's one need of both of ours that won't be met. Arnie will feel pity for us, not jealousy."

"To hell with Arnie."

"Amen to that. However, you are finishing college."

"No, I'm not."

"Yes, you are."

"How come I have to finish college and you don't have to finish law school?"

"Because a college degree will make you feel better about yourself and might even help your career. I want that for you and I'll keep pushing until you take care of it."

"For crying out loud, why?"

She got right into his face. "Because I love you, you dolt."

"Are you about to strangle me with a piece of something intimate?" he couldn't help but ask.

"It's a temptation, believe me."

She held her eyes steady as she looked right into his and he realized she was waiting for something. "Oh, honey, I love you, too, and I want you in so many ways I can't even count them."

"We'll be broke for a long time to come," she warned.

"I don't care. We'll get by."

G.T. brought his arms around her and hugged her to him. Claire squeezed back and enthusiastically returned his kiss when G.T. sought out her lips. "You know what?" he asked.

"What?" she obligingly inquired.

"I think you were the source of my malcontent all along, not my job."

"I caused you to be *malcontent?*"

"Not having you did," he corrected. "And now that I do have you, I expect a real feeling of euphoria next time I write out a parking ticket."

"You do, huh?"

"Oh, yeah. In fact, I'm going to practice feeling euphoric right now by parking your sexy little body on the bed in there. Then I'm going to serve you every citation in the book."

"I can hardly wait."
"You don't have to."
And she didn't.

* * * * *

Silhouette ROMANCE

COMING NEXT MONTH

#1048 ANYTHING FOR DANNY—Carla Cassidy
Under the Mistletoe—Fabulous Fathers
Danny Morgan had one wish this Christmas—to reunite his divorced parents. But Sherri and Luke Morgan needed more than their son's hopes to bring them together. They needed to rediscover their long-lost love.

#1049 TO WED AT CHRISTMAS—Helen R. Myers
Under the Mistletoe
Nothing could stop David Shepherd and Harmony Martin from falling in love—though their feuding families struggled to keep them apart. Would it take a miracle to get them married?

#1050 MISS SCROOGE—Toni Collins
Under the Mistletoe
"Bah, humbug" was all lonely Casey Tucker had to say about the holidays. But that was before handsome Gabe Wheeler gave her the most wonderful Christmas gift of all....

#1051 BELIEVING IN MIRACLES—Linda Varner
Under the Mistletoe—Mr. Right, Inc.
Andy Fulbright missed family life, and Honey Truman needed a father for her son. Their convenient marriage fulfilled their common needs, but would love fulfill their dreams?

#1052 A COWBOY FOR CHRISTMAS—Stella Bagwell
Under the Mistletoe
Spending the holidays with cowboy Chance Delacroix was a joy Lucinda Lambert knew couldn't last. She was a woman on the run, and leaving was the only way to keep Chance out of danger.

#1053 SURPRISE PACKAGE—Lynn Bulock
Under the Mistletoe
Miranda Dalton needed a miracle to save A Caring Place shelter. What she got was Jared Tarkett. What could a sexy drifter teach *her* about life, love and commitment?

MILLION DOLLAR SWEEPSTAKES (III)

No purchase necessary. To enter, follow the directions published. Method of entry may vary. For eligibility, entries must be received no later than March 31, 1996. No liability is assumed for printing errors, lost, late or misdirected entries. Odds of winning are determined by the number of eligible entries distributed and received. Prizewinners will be determined no later than June 30, 1996.

Sweepstakes open to residents of the U.S. (except Puerto Rico), Canada, Europe and Taiwan who are 18 years of age or older. All applicable laws and regulations apply. Sweepstakes offer void wherever prohibited by law. Values of all prizes are in U.S. currency. This sweepstakes is presented by Torstar Corp., its subsidiaries and affiliates, in conjunction with book, merchandise and/or product offerings. For a copy of the Official Rules send a self-addressed, stamped envelope (WA residents need not affix return postage) to: MILLION DOLLAR SWEEPSTAKES (III) Rules, P.O. Box 4573, Blair, NE 68009, USA.

EXTRA BONUS PRIZE DRAWING

No purchase necessary. The Extra Bonus Prize will be awarded in a random drawing to be conducted no later than 5/30/96 from among all entries received. To qualify, entries must be received by 3/31/96 and comply with published directions. Drawing open to residents of the U.S. (except Puerto Rico), Canada, Europe and Taiwan who are 18 years of age or older. All applicable laws and regulations apply; offer void wherever prohibited by law. Odds of winning are dependent upon number of eligibile entries received. Prize is valued in U.S. currency. The offer is presented by Torstar Corp., its subsidiaries and affiliates in conjunction with book, merchandise and/or product offering. For a copy of the Official Rules governing this sweepstakes, send a self-addressed, stamped envelope (WA residents need not affix return postage) to: Extra Bonus Prize Drawing Rules, P.O. Box 4590, Blair, NE 68009, USA.

SWP-S1194

JINGLE BELLS, WEDDING BELLS:
Silhouette's Christmas Collection for 1994

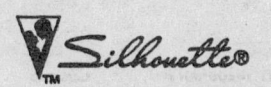

Christmas Wish List

*To beat the crowds at the malls and get the perfect present for *everyone*, even that snoopy Mrs. Smith next door!

*To get through the holiday parties without running my panty hose.

*To bake cookies, decorate the house and serve the perfect Christmas dinner—just like the women in all those magazines.

*To sit down, curl up and read my Silhouette Christmas stories!

Join *New York Times* bestselling author Nora Roberts, along with popular writers Barbara Boswell, Myrna Temte and Elizabeth August, as we celebrate the joys of Christmas—and the magic of marriage—with

JINGLE BELLS, WEDDING BELLS

Silhouette's Christmas Collection for 1994.

Silhouette®

JBWB

Available in November from Silhouette Romance...

WEDDING WAGER

by Sandra Steffen

Three sexy, single brothers bet they'll never say "I do." But the Harris boys are about to discover that their vows of bachelorhood don't stand a chance against the forces of love!

You fell in love with Mitch Harris in BACHELOR DADDY (8/94).

Now it's time that brother Kyle finds the woman of his dreams. It all begins when Kyle catches the garter and lovely single mom Clarissa Cohagan catches the bouquet in BACHELOR AT THE WEDDING (11/94).

And watch for Taylor's story, EXPECTANT BACHELOR, available 1/95.

Don't miss WEDDING WAGER,
only from *Silhouette* ROMANCE™

If you missed *Bachelor Daddy*, order your copy now by sending your name, address, zip or postal code, along with a check or money order (please do not send cash) for $2.75, ($3.25 in Canada) plus 75¢ postage and handling ($1.00 in Canada), payable to Silhouette Books, to:

In the U.S.	In Canada
Silhouette Books	Silhouette Books
3010 Walden Ave.	P. O. Box 636
P. O. Box 9077	Fort Erie, Ontario
Buffalo, NY 14269-9077	L2A 5X3

*Please specify book title with your order.
Canadian residents add applicable federal and provincial taxes.

SRSS2

HARLEQUIN®   **SUNDAYS ON CBS HARLEQUIN MOVIES WATCH FOR THEM**   **Silhouette®**

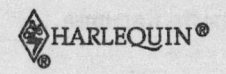

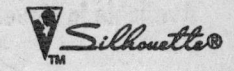

The movie event of the season can be the reading event of the year!

Lights... The lights go on in October when CBS presents Harlequin/Silhouette Sunday Matinee Movies. These four movies are based on bestselling Harlequin and Silhouette novels.

Camera... As the cameras roll, be the first to read the original novels the movies are based on!

Action... Through this offer, you can have these books sent directly to you! Just fill in the order form below and you could be reading the books...before the movie!

48288-4	Treacherous Beauties by Cheryl Emerson $3.99 U.S./$4.50 CAN.	☐
83305-9	Fantasy Man by Sharon Green $3.99 U.S./$4.50 CAN.	☐
48289-2	A Change of Place by Tracy Sinclair $3.99 U.S./$4.50CAN.	☐
83306-7	Another Woman by Margot Dalton $3.99 U.S./$4.50 CAN.	☐

TOTAL AMOUNT	$
POSTAGE & HANDLING	$
($1.00 for one book, 50¢ for each additional)	
APPLICABLE TAXES*	$ _____
TOTAL PAYABLE	$ _____
(check or money order—please do not send cash)	

To order, complete this form and send it, along with a check or money order for the total above, payable to Harlequin Books, to: **In the U.S.:** 3010 Walden Avenue, P.O. Box 9047, Buffalo, NY 14269-9047; **In Canada:** P.O. Box 613, Fort Erie, Ontario, L2A 5X3.

Name: _____

Address: _____ City: _____

State/Prov.: _____ Zip/Postal Code: _____

*New York residents remit applicable sales taxes.
Canadian residents remit applicable GST and provincial taxes.   CBSPR

"HOORAY FOR HOLLYWOOD" SWEEPSTAKES

HERE'S HOW THE SWEEPSTAKES WORKS

OFFICIAL RULES — NO PURCHASE NECESSARY

To enter, complete an Official Entry Form or hand print on a 3" x 5" card the words "HOORAY FOR HOLLYWOOD", your name and address and mail your entry in the pre-addressed envelope (if provided) or to: "Hooray for Hollywood" Sweepstakes, P.O. Box 9076, Buffalo, NY 14269-9076 or "Hooray for Hollywood" Sweepstakes, P.O. Box 637, Fort Erie, Ontario L2A 5X3. Entries must be sent via First Class Mail and be received no later than 12/31/94. No liability is assumed for lost, late or misdirected mail.

Winners will be selected in random drawings to be conducted no later than January 31, 1995 from all eligible entries received.

Grand Prize: A 7-day/6-night trip for 2 to Los Angeles, CA including round trip air transportation from commercial airport nearest winner's residence, accommodations at the Regent Beverly Wilshire Hotel, free rental car, and $1,000 spending money. (Approximate prize value which will vary dependent upon winner's residence: $5,400.00 U.S.); 500 Second Prizes: A pair of "Hollywood Star" sunglasses (prize value: $9.95 U.S. each). Winner selection is under the supervision of D.L. Blair, Inc., an independent judging organization, whose decisions are final. Grand Prize travelers must sign and return a release of liability prior to traveling. Trip must be taken by 2/1/96 and is subject to airline schedules and accommodations availability.

Sweepstakes offer is open to residents of the U.S. (except Puerto Rico) and Canada who are 18 years of age or older, except employees and immediate family members of Harlequin Enterprises, Ltd., its affiliates, subsidiaries, and all agencies, entities or persons connected with the use, marketing or conduct of this sweepstakes. All federal, state, provincial, municipal and local laws apply. Offer void wherever prohibited by law. Taxes and/or duties are the sole responsibility of the winners. Any litigation within the province of Quebec respecting the conduct and awarding of prizes may be submitted to the Regie des loteries et courses du Quebec. All prizes will be awarded; winners will be notified by mail. No substitution of prizes are permitted. Odds of winning are dependent upon the number of eligible entries received.

Potential grand prize winner must sign and return an Affidavit of Eligibility within 30 days of notification. In the event of non-compliance within this time period, prize may be awarded to an alternate winner. Prize notification returned as undeliverable may result in the awarding of prize to an alternate winner. By acceptance of their prize, winners consent to use of their names, photographs, or likenesses for purpose of advertising, trade and promotion on behalf of Harlequin Enterprises, Ltd., without further compensation unless prohibited by law. A Canadian winner must correctly answer an arithmetical skill-testing question in order to be awarded the prize.

For a list of winners (available after 2/28/95), send a separate stamped, self-addressed envelope to: Hooray for Hollywood Sweepstakes 3252 Winners, P.O. Box 4200, Blair, NE 68009.

CBSRLS

OFFICIAL ENTRY COUPON
"Hooray for Hollywood"
SWEEPSTAKES!

Yes, I'd love to win the Grand Prize — a vacation in Hollywood — or one of 500 pairs of "sunglasses of the stars"! Please enter me in the sweepstakes!

This entry must be received by December 31, 1994.
Winners will be notified by January 31, 1995.

Name _____

Address _____ Apt. _____

City _____

State/Prov. _____ Zip/Postal Code _____

Daytime phone number _____
(area code)

Mail all entries to: Hooray for Hollywood Sweepstakes,
P.O. Box 9076, Buffalo, NY 14269-9076.
In Canada, mail to: Hooray for Hollywood Sweepstakes,
P.O. Box 637, Fort Erie, ON L2A 5X3.

KCH

OFFICIAL ENTRY COUPON
"Hooray for Hollywood"
SWEEPSTAKES!

Yes, I'd love to win the Grand Prize — a vacation in Hollywood — or one of 500 pairs of "sunglasses of the stars"! Please enter me in the sweepstakes!

This entry must be received by December 31, 1994.
Winners will be notified by January 31, 1995.

Name _____

Address _____ Apt. _____

City _____

State/Prov. _____ Zip/Postal Code _____

Daytime phone number _____
(area code)

Mail all entries to: Hooray for Hollywood Sweepstakes,
P.O. Box 9076, Buffalo, NY 14269-9076.
In Canada, mail to: Hooray for Hollywood Sweepstakes,
P.O. Box 637, Fort Erie, ON L2A 5X3.

KCH